KEEPING HIM

THE ROYALS OF AVALONE - INHERITANCE: VICTORIA
PART 3

E.V. DARCY

Edited by
COOKIELYNN PUBLISHING SERVICES

Copyright © 2021 E. V. Darcy

Cover Design © 2021 Victoria Smith

All rights reserved.

This is a work of fiction. Names, characters, businesses, places, events, and incidents are either the products of the author's imagination or used in a fictitious manner. Any resemblance to actual persons, living or dead, or actual events is purely coincidental.

All rights reserved. No part of this publication may be reproduced, distributed, or transmitted in any form or by any means, including photocopying, recording, or other electronic or mechanical methods, without the prior written permission of the publisher, except in the case of brief quotations embodied in critical reviews and certain other non-commercial uses permitted by copyright law. For permission requests, write to the publisher, addressed "Attention: Permissions Coordinator," at the address below.

Info@evdarcy.com

For all those who will fight for their Happily Ever After

It takes hundreds of hours and thousands of dollars to produce a novel, so thank you for buying this book and supporting an author's dream.

If you got this book for free (outside of your local library) then this book has been pirated against the author's wishes.

Please enjoy immersing yourself into the world of Avalone and falling in love with the people of this unique nation.

King Richard VIII

Grand Duke Harold
- Prince Alistair of Avalone

Princess Helena
- Prince Spencer
- Prince Adam
- Princess Caroline

Duke Alfred
- Prince Leopold
- Prince John

Duke Frederick
- Prince Arthur
- Princess Rebecca
- Princess Francessca

Duke Augustus
- Prince George — Princess Grace
  The first surviving Royal Twins

Princess Amelia
- Princess Jane
- Princess Elizabeth
- Princess Louise
- Prince Hugh

Princess Melinda
- Lady Victoria
- Lady Henrietta
- Lady Philippa
- Lady Alexandra

CHAPTER ONE

*T*he messages kept coming.

Cormac had left his phone behind while they'd gone away on their honeymoon, as had Victoria. They'd enjoyed two weeks on the Royal Yacht, only reachable via the on-board satellite phone which he'd used twice a day to check up on James—who'd had the time of his life with *Auntie Alexi*. At the time, Cormac had had no idea what the girl was doing to entertain his brother but had been grateful. However, not so much on his return home.

He'd come back to find his brother covered in bruises from adventures such as paintballing, learning how to skateboard, and other insane activities she'd had the two of them doing. However, he had to grudgingly admit the photographs she'd sent to his phone were adorable.

But that was when he'd seen *the messages*. Several a day had come through to his phone while he'd been gone. More images of Cormac posing almost naked, one that suggested he definitely was. The worst was an image taken from a security camera of Geri oiling his shoulders and back where he couldn't reach. It looked highly sexual, even if it was the furthest thing from it; in fact, he was sure the images were from his last night at the club. He was never more thankful for refusing the fluffing service she had to offer the strippers than he was at that moment.

He did as Marcus said and messaged the Guard with simply, *7-7-7.*

'Happy to be home?' Victoria asked as she came into the bedroom of the penthouse they were still renting, kicking off her high heels before standing before him. 'You know, we have the whole place to ourselves tonight. No James until tomorrow afternoon.'

'What are you thinking?'

'I was thinking,' she said with a wicked smirk. 'That we could christen a few more of the rooms here.'

'Really?' Cormac looked towards the doors that led out to their private sitting room. 'Do you think they're jealous?'

'That these rooms keep getting all the sex? Most definitely,' she said with a solemn nod. 'How about we take a swim?' Cormac's cock instantly twitched at the idea. Since their wedding night, she'd had a bit of a penchant for outdoor experiences. The pool and the sun lounging deck on the yacht had become her favoured places for their fun. The possibility of them being seen was a thrill for her, even if the crew knew that when he'd told them they wanted *complete* privacy, they weren't to be *anywhere* above deck, not just on the parts they were enjoying. It was the titillation of the idea of someone watching or overhearing that drove her wild. The fact their pool here was in the open—even if they were at the top of one of the tallest towers in all the land—was obviously giving her the same ideas.

'Want to go *skinny dipping?*' His fingers slipped under the thin straps of her summer dress before slowly pushing them over her shoulders and down her arms. She breathed in deeply as the dress fell from her torso, exposing her breasts to the air. He lowered his head to hers and kissed her lips before moving to her neck.

She moaned as he kissed just below her ear, her hands grasping his arms to keep herself steady as she turned into his touch. His fingers gently stroked up her side, causing her to shiver, her breath turning ragged as he lightly skimmed the side of her breast.

'Cormac,' she hissed breathlessly, arching her back slightly, trying to get him to touch her properly. 'Please.'

'Now, now, princess,' he whispered in her ear as his other hand reached up to her hair to undo the clip that held her locks in place. 'We're not at the pool yet, isn't that where you want me to *fuck* you?' She moaned wantonly at his words. 'Isn't that where you want your sweet prince to turn you from a royal lady into a common *whore?*'

'Oh, God!' she whimpered before grabbing his face and bringing it to hers. She kissed him with such ferocity that it took Cormac a second to respond in kind. He pulled her against his body, holding her tightly as he poured every ounce of his desire, his love for her, into the moment.

He pushed the dress over her hips, before slipping his fingers into the sides of her knickers and pushing them down to join the discarded dress.

Her hands moved to his belt, quickly unbuckling it while he worked on his fly. They weren't going to make it to the pool, but he'd ensure he make it up to her afterwards.

'Cormac,' she said against his lips. 'The window.'

'What?' he asked, glancing towards the glass. The curtains were open; did she suddenly want them shut?

'I want you to take me up against it.'

'Oh, you are—'

The shrill ringing of his phone made the two of them jump. He frowned down at where he'd thrown it on the bed when she'd come in. *Private number* flashed on the screen, and he ignored it, pulling Victoria to him and capturing her lips once more. But when the phone rang out, it started all over again.

The two of them groaned.

'Just answer the thing,' she said as she turned around. He grabbed the phone, hating the damn device even more, and swiped up so hard he thought he could crack the glass on, before all but shouting *what?* into it.

He watched Victoria sashay her way towards the window, dressed only in her stiletto sandals. She reached the glass pane and turned around, resting her back against the glass. Her hand slithered down her torso between her breasts, moving down past her navel and into her small thatch of hair that crowned her glory.

'What?' he snapped again, having completely missed whatever it was the person calling him had said. He was enraptured by her fingers moving within her folds, her little gasps of pleasure as she stared back at him with lust filled eyes. She bit her lip as she tried to bite back a moan, but the wanton sound slipped between them and went straight to his straining cock. 'I'm rather busy right now.'

'I said, you're late on your payment.' Cormac froze as he finally recognised O'Malley's voice. 'Now put your bride down, tuck your cock away, and get your arse downstairs. I'm waiting.' The line went dead.

He slowly dropped the phone from his ear, staring at Victoria as she posed in front of the window, the sun framing her as a silhouette made it all the more sensual and meant to stoke the fire of desire within him, but at that moment, all it filled him with was ice.

'Get away from the window,' he growled at her, racing forward and seizing her by the arm to haul her from the glass.

'Cormac!' Victoria gasped as he grabbed the curtains and

pulled them across the window, plunging the room into darkness. 'What on earth—'

'Someone was watching,' he barked, turning away from her as he tucked his now very limp length back inside his boxers and refastened his trousers.

'They were what?' she cried, rushing for her robe, and throwing it around her. 'How?'

'I dunno,' he answered honestly. 'I'm going to go and find out what's going on. I won't be long.' He didn't look back as he strode from the room, cursing up a storm.

He searched for Marcus' number as he pressed the button to call the lift.

'Hello?' came Marcus' voice over the line.

'We got a *big* problem,' was all he was able to say before the lift arrived and he hung up.

CORMAC FUMED ALL THE WAY DOWN TO THE LOBBY. THE hotel's other guests quickly moved out of his way or stared at him from their seats as he stormed through the reception area, shoving the doors open with the palm of his hand. The doormen jumped at the force the door swung open, scrambling to catch it in time before it pivoted all the way and it hit the wall.

He had no idea how he knew the limousine sitting in front of the building was waiting for him; he just *knew*. He all but snarled as he approached the shiny, black car, the door opening before he reached it and the tall goon he'd shoved down last time O'Malley had paid him a visit was the one to climb out. He held the door open for Cormac who stopped and glared at the man before he dipped his head and slid onto the leather seat. The bruiser followed him a moment later.

An orange glow from the interior lights lit up the back of the carThis time, the back of the long vehicle, highlighting the rotund, little man that was O'Malley. He faced him in the centre of the seat behind the driver. The only interiors of limousines Cormac had previously seen were the party-types that turned up to the club, but this... This was nice. A mahogany bar ran along one side of the car opposite a length of seats where another thug—this one rather stocky—sat staring at him. Tall-goon settled into the seat next to Cormac, and he knew it was so the man could grab him if he tried to get out before O'Malley gave him permission to leave.

'Nice of *His Lordship* to deign to join us,' O'Malley said around his ever-present cigar. 'I hope you enjoyed the honeymoon.' The two men who accompanied their boss sniggered.

'Look, I don't know what you want with me. I fulfilled my side of things.'

'Kid, you got a lot of nerve, but I don't think you understand the extent of the situation. See, *I* gave you something, and *you* gave me nothing. So, you owe me. Now, I have given you *plenty* of chances to make this right, so I'm going to give you one more and then I'm going to start making you wish you'd done as I asked.'

'You're going to break my legs?' Cormac crossed his arms and sat back in his seat. 'Going to look a bit odd if I randomly turn up with two broken legs.'

O'Malley put his cigar between his lips and grabbed his phone from his inside pocket. He said nothing as he unlocked the device and searched for something on it. Cormac was about to roll his eyes, thinking it was going to be yet another picture of him when his own voice rang out loud and clear in the confines of the limo.

'My car alarm started going off and so I ran downstairs. When

I opened the door, I saw this fat bastard on his knees leaning over Lady Victoria who was out cold on the floor—'

O'Malley pressed the screen and Cormac's voice stopped. The fucker had taped their first conversation when Cormac had told him exactly *how* he and Victoria had first met. The story they'd told the world would be quickly unravelled if that got out. O'Malley watched him expectantly.

'You know,' Cormac said, hoping he looked and sounded as unimpressed as he thought he did. 'I've made rather good friends with the Head of the Royal Guard. In fact, he's tracking my phone as we speak.'

O'Malley's eyes narrowed at Cormac.

'I suggest you stop trying to blackmail me and that you quit texting me. All you have are a few pictures of me semi-naked, which, while embarrassing, would probably only raise my stock in the public eye.'

'I can blow your little fairy tale apart with this—'

'Nah.' Cormac waved away the man's words with one hand and turned to stare out of the window as if the view was far more interesting. 'All that says is that Victoria recognised where she was that night and came to try and find me to save her. Yes, it doesn't look as neat as it could, but you can't release the whole thing without your own voice being part of it either.' Cormac sniffed, turning back to the man. 'So, you can release just that part and we'll be able to talk it away; we'll do a few photo shoots just to make everyone fawn over them. Perhaps, we'll do it in swimwear so that I'm mostly *naked*.' He hoped that got the point across of how the pictures wouldn't really be much of a hindrance. 'Or you have to release it in full, with your voice on it. And I have to say, Marcus Walker is *very* interested in you right now.'

'Get out.' The car immediately stopped its slow drive.

'We are *done*,' Cormac reiterated, opening the car door.

'Oh, you so are, kid,' O'Malley replied just as the car door shut behind him.

The words left a bad taste in Cormac's mouth as he watched the car pull away from the curb before turning left and disappearing. A few minutes later, his phone rang again.

'Yes?'

'We're tracking him now. Good job.'

'Make sure this really is over and done with, Marcus,' he said as he began to walk back to the hotel. 'I don't want Victoria thinking she has another stalker out there, or that she's got no privacy because of *me*. Also, he's got a recording of me.' He explained the full situation to the guard.

'Leave that with me,' Marcus said. 'I can put out a few notices to editors across the country. Nothing like that will be printed or broadcast.'

'Doesn't stop the internet,' Cormac told him before hanging up the call as he arrived back at the hotel. He glanced up, following the sleek glass all the way to the very top where he knew his wife would be worrying herself sick. Taking a deep breath, he stepped inside and began working on his story to tell her.

CHAPTER TWO

Victoria sighed and rubbed her eyes, pushing the tablet away to give herself a break for a few minutes.

'What's up?' Cormac asked as he walked into the usually bright and airy sitting room. 'Why're the curtains all closed?' He turned to stare at her. As she often was, she was tucked in the corner of the room behind the overly large desk, curled up on the generous chair that went with it. Usually, she was bestowed the gift of a beautiful view over the city leading out towards the bay, but today she'd pulled the curtains tight and the room was lit by one lamp on the other side.

'Too bright. Got a headache' she muttered. She cringed as Cormac sighed, seeing right through her lie. She didn't want to admit it, but knowing people were sending up drones to try and capture them going about their lives had scared her far more than she thought rational. She'd been through so many scarier scenarios, but there was always a weak link in an elaborate crime, such as a kidnapping—that was how so many attempts against her had been foiled. That, and a stalker was spotted before they could become a threat to her —well, save for that *one* time.

However, someone desperately trying to snap a picture just to sell to the media... She shuddered at the thought. Criminals needed punishment and rehabilitation; stalkers needed psychological help. How did you stop someone who was simply motivated by making a quick crown?

Cormac put his cup down on the coffee table and scrubbed his hands over his face before turning back to her.

'Victoria, you can't lock yourself away.' He had desperately been trying to reassure her that everything was okay since the moment he'd returned from his meeting with Marcus. He looked like a guilty puppy every time he found her squirrelled away somewhere she knew *they* couldn't get easy access to. She hadn't used the pool since, hadn't allowed James to either, much to the child's annoyance.

She straightened in the chair again and pulled the tablet back towards her, purposefully scrolling through the images as if nothing were wrong save for Cormac's assumptions.

'I'm not. I'm looking at houses so we can get *out* of here. But nothing's right,' she said despondently. 'It's either too big or too small, or there's not enough privacy, or it's too far away from Highbourne—James starts school on *Tuesday* and unless you want him to board there—'

'No way.' He had been very outspoken on such a matter.

'Then we really need to find somewhere quickly or he's going to have over an hour to travel each way, every day.' She sighed and rubbed her hand over her forehead. 'It's all my fault. I put it off for too long. I should have been searching *before* we got married—'

'Victoria,' he began as he made his way to her. 'You have found, like, a *hundred* houses and I have said yes to about twenty-five of them—*you're* the one who keeps saying no.'

She turned the chair and levelled a look at him over the

top of the tablet, hoping he'd stop in his tracks. He was far too distracting when he got near. Or when he wasn't, and he started getting undressed. Or working out. Or lounging on the couch watching films…

She shook herself of her thoughts and narrowed her eyes accusingly at him.

'You said *yes* to a three-bed semi-detached on a *housing estate*,' she reminded him. 'It wasn't even for sale. I just threw it in there to test you and you *failed*. Spectacularly.'

'Princess.' He dropped his voice, and it sent a shiver of desire down her spine. That usually only meant one thing; he was going to distract her. She quickly spun her chair around, but it was no good. His hands gently rested on her shoulders as he dipped his head and pressed a kiss against her bare neck. She couldn't help the sigh that slipped from her lips. Or the smirk that spread across them. She'd taken to wearing her hair up more and more just to get him to do such a thing.

'What have I told you about wearing your hair like this?' He popped open the clip that held her twist in place. 'It gives you a headache, makes you grumpy, and then you'll never pick a place.'

Her eyes fluttered closed as he nibbled at her neck and she dropped her shoulders to give him better access to *that* spot he'd somehow managed to find. His lips pressed against the juncture of her neck and shoulder and she didn't even try and hold back the moan that fell from her lips as a shiver of pleasure rippled through her body.

'Cormac, please,' she murmured half-heartedly. 'We need to find a *home*.' He sighed against her, but pressed one last kiss to her skin before looking at the tablet she still held firmly.

'What was wrong with the last one I liked again?'

'It only had four bedrooms.'

'There are only three of us,' he pointed out. Victoria huffed as she dropped her head back to peer up at him.

'There are *now*,' she reminded him. 'But when we have a baby, there will be four of us.' He didn't meet her eyes; instead, he kept them fixed on the picture on the screen as he nodded his head and pressed his lips together.

Victoria cursed herself.

She could get lost in his touch and kisses all she liked, could listen to him talk for hours about anything in his deep, sexy timbre. She could drool over his hot body whenever he revealed it, and could ache inside as she watched him play the father figure so brilliantly to James, but none of that negated the fact that this wasn't a marriage for love.

He was here because she was paying him. He was here to solve a problem she had. And she knew that no matter how kind, generous, and sweet Cormac was to her—and no matter how much she knew she could easily fall in love with the man behind her—he only saw her as a friend at best. A friend with benefits. *Lots* of benefits.

His brow was probably lined because he was trying to fathom how to point out the fact that once she had a baby, their time was at an end and they wouldn't *need* four bedrooms because there wouldn't be *four* of them there. It would be her and their baby.

Oh yes, they'd have joint access—as per their agreement—but that simply meant she could probably get away with just three bedrooms.

'Let me guess,' he said, leaning forward and swiping at the screen to change the picture. 'You want a spare room for guests to stay with us?'

Victoria released her breath and looked down at the screen. The image became blurry and she had to blink back the unexpected wetness in her eyes at the fact he *didn't* point out such a fact. It didn't make it any less true, but it gave her a sliver of hope that he wouldn't pack up the moment she got a positive pregnancy test.

'Well, think about it,' she said and cleared her throat. 'I have three sisters and you have your friends; if we throw a party, we're quite a drive from the city, and wouldn't you like having the option for them to stay over?'

'That's what couches and floors are for,' he said without a thought as he reached over her and plucked the tablet from her hands.

'The *floor?*' she asked aghast. He nodded. 'You're a caveman.'

'I'm a poor man.'

'Not anymore.'

'How many properties did she send over today?' he asked, turning away and heading to where he'd been going to set up camp before he'd spied her.

'Just six,' she said miserably, resting her cheek in her hand. 'We're going to run out of options soon.'

'You mean *you're* going to.'

Victoria held her breath again. Had he been looking at places on his own? Had he picked one in preparation for when he left her? The idea made her heart sink and her stomach churn.

'What's wrong with this one? Looks nice—eight bedrooms, so more than enough—and it has a *pool.*' He waggled his brows at her and a deep swell of relief flooded her body before flushing red hot at the memories of their honeymoon. She'd enjoyed their freedom for those ten days very much—nothing to plan for or do save soak up the sun, frolic in the sea, and make love to her new husband. She had hoped their easy camaraderie and the heat between them would continue upon their return, and she knew Cormac was more than willing, but after the drone incident, she felt as if they were constantly being watched and she *hated* it.

She'd not been able to get into the *mood* properly since. She'd asked Merryweather to take a couple of the paintings out of their bedroom because their stares made her skin crawl.

Cormac hadn't said anything, but he hadn't tried to initiate sex since that day.

She sighed.

'Indoor or outdoor?' she queried—indoor might work. She stood up and went to join him on the couch to peek. She had to admit, it sounded good so far.

'*Both.*' He grinned, and she couldn't help the small smile in return. That only seemed to make his brighter.

'Oh, no.' Her shoulders sagged in disappointment as Cormac flicked to the next image. 'Look at those stables, they're a mess. We can't live there.'

Cormac paused, his whole body going still before he slowly turned to her. 'We… What?'

'Pardon?' She blinked, unsure what his problem was.

'The *stables* mean we can't buy a house?'

'Just look at them, Cormac. They're terrible!'

'And are you planning on keeping horses?'

She glanced up at him in confusion. 'No.'

'Then what's the problem?'

'Well… they're… an eyesore.' She hesitated, suddenly unsure of her protest. She recalled his flat, how small it was, how there was only one bedroom between he and James, and that he'd slept in the living room on a sofa-bed. She was being a completely spoilt cow, but she just wanted the *best* for them. Perhaps if she could find the *perfect* house, he might decide to stay. She closed her mind off to such thoughts; she didn't need him, didn't need to be hurt more than she knew she was going to be when he up and left her.

'They're not far from the house—look, you can see them from the outdoor pool.'

'So, we do them up, turn them into workshops or…' He

smiled at whatever thought popped into his head. 'What about guest *suites*? Then you can invite anyone you want to stay over, and they don't need to be underfoot.'

Huh. She'd never thought of converting something before. She leaned in close to him and he threw his arm around her, pulling her against his chest as they continued to flick through the pictures. She supposed they weren't *too* bad. They looked structurally okay, and they could put in a few windows here and there, maybe some skylights in the hayloft above. Oh, they could theme them!

'Maybe we could go and see it,' she said cautiously. 'You know just to make sure they're not completely decrepit.'

'Yeah?'

'Yes.' She nodded, rubbing her cheek against his t-shirt. 'I'll make the arrangement with Kirstie tomorrow.'

'Good girl,' he said as he pressed the power button on the top of the device. He tossed it on to the chair nearby, much to her horror. But she didn't get a chance to protest, because as soon as the tablet was out of his hand, he pulled her up and over his lap.

'Now, with eight bedrooms, that's a lot of christenings,' he said with a completely straight face. He waited for her, kept his hands on the couch in case she wanted to bolt from him. She stared at him, her heart fluttering in her chest; unsure if it should race in fear of someone spying on them or dance in happiness and excitement at the idea of making love to the man beneath her.

'Do you... Do you think that we'll need to practice?' she asked warily, still unsure she'd be able to actually play along. That was until Cormac's smile broke wide across his face.

'Oh, yes, princess.' His hands gently stroked up her thighs. 'If we're going to ensure that we give our home our best performance, we're going to have to practice a *lot*.'

Our home. The words made her heart beat wildly for a

completely different reason. One she chose to ignore as she smiled back at him, before lowering her head to his.

Victoria had to admit, it was perfect. The house was old, a manor home from the late 17th century, probably owned by a lord or baron at some point. At least someone far too low down the royal line for the house to have been taken into the crown estates when the family had decided to vacate it.

It had a perfectly central porch for the old heavy wooden door, the symmetrical wings on either side of the main entrance were home to glorious stone-framed double-storey bay windows, and rising from the north side of the house, was a four-storey tower but she had no idea what that was for!

As they came around the long winding driveway, through the thicket of trees that lined it, Victoria twisted her fingers into her trousers to stop from throwing herself at the window to get a better look.

Beautiful purple wisteria crept up the walls at the front of the building, winding its way around the tops of the bay windows and arching over the main entrance, creating a curtain of purple for them to walk through when they arrived.

'The roof is going to need some work,' Cormac murmured next to her. Victoria blinked; she'd been so captivated by the beauty of the house she'd forgotten she wasn't alone.

'Yes,' Kirstie's voice came over the car's speaker. With Cormac now riding in the back of the Rolls-Royce with her, her assistant was now sequestered in the front seat next to Toby. Maybe they needed to get a different vehicle? 'It will also need extensive redecoration inside. The pools will both need to be checked—I fear at least the outdoor one is leaking from the reports. And then there's the...'

But Victoria stopped listening again as she took in the breath-taking old home as they drove along the road that never seemed to end. It was set on a slight hill; the small moat that had once surrounded it long dried out, but it only added to the depth of the gardens that grew wild and unkempt. They were going to need a lot of work, she noted, but the idea of planning her own garden after watching the royal gardeners doing the same thing repeatedly for years gave her a little thrill.

'Have there been any additions?' she found herself asking her assistant, unable to take her eyes from the building.

'The orangery was added at some point in the 18th century, but the house stands as it did otherwise. It was built in a U-shape with a courtyard open to the south. The entrance is on the west-side, the tower...'

Victoria switched off again as they finally made it to the entrance of the building. She didn't even wait for Toby to fully stop the car, let alone open the door for her, as she was already stepping out of the vehicle as he applied the handbrake.

'Victoria!' Cormac chided as he flung open his own door and hurried around to where she stood gazing up at the building.

'How much again?' she asked breathlessly. She didn't care how much it cost. This was it. This was going to be their home.

'Five million.'

Her head snapped around to look at her assistant who was just jogging around the car to join them. '*Crowns*? No, that's *insane*.' Okay, so it mattered a *little* how much it cost. 'Who the hell is the seller?'

Kirstie hurriedly flicked through the papers in the folder she held, her eyes scanning each page for the information she needed. Victoria knew when she found it; her face twisted up into disgust.

'Oh, that explains it.' The private sectary sighed before meeting Victoria's expectant gaze. 'A Mr Bob Gallo. He's an American.'

'Let me guess; he inherited it decades ago, never lived here, and now wants to make a killing on the current price of gold which skyrocketed last week?' Kirstie checked through the papers again, before nodding her head.

'He's never going to get the asking price on this. Are you sure it's not US dollars?' Kirstie shook her head. 'Doesn't he realise that properties just don't sell for prices like that here? Did he get crowns mixed up with slivers? Because I'd pay five million slivers right now for it.'

'We haven't gone inside yet,' Cormac reminded her. He was right, but she didn't care if they walked through that door and all they found was a shell, she *wanted* this house. The location alone, she realised as she turned and looked out over the fields below them, would be worth every bit... for the price she was thinking.

'How much land is with it?' she asked Kirstie as she shielded her eyes from the sun with her hand and took in the beautiful vista beyond the jungle of a garden. There was just greenery for miles around. The landscape was filled with well-kept fields full of crops that would be ready to harvest soon. Dotting the view every so often were copses of trees and about midway down her view to the horizon, there appeared to be a body of water peeking out from what looked to be a good-sized woodland or forest beginning. She wondered if it was the start of the Golden Hills National Park; if so, then that was probably Lake Earling which only made her smile brighter. That was where her mother and father had brought them as children for weekends of sailing and horse riding during term-time. The idea she'd be able to do the same with her own children made her chest swell with joy.

'Fifty-two acres.'

'That's not much,' Victoria said, her brow marring with confusion as she tried to fathom how far away the lake was and if there was the possibility of a private mooring.

Cormac spluttered at her side. 'You want *more*? What the hell are you going to do with *fifty-two* acres as it is?'

Victoria rolled her eyes as she turned back to her husband. At that reaction, she wasn't going to tell him she was hoping for a bit of the lake all to herself. He'd tell her how greedy and selfish it was. And he'd be right, which was why she said instead, 'Cormac, houses like these came with acres upon acres of land.'

'And fifty-two acres isn't *acre upon acre*?'

'They had hundreds, with farms and often whole villages attached to them.'

'They were handed back to the Crown in the late nineteenth century when the property was first sold by the Denyer family,' Kirstie said, glancing through her file again. 'Apparently, it was part of the agreement for Lord Denyer to actually be able to sell it. That and giving up his title. Or so the local myth goes.'

Victoria gave Cormac a look that screamed, *Ha! So there!* before she focused her attention on Kirstie, beaming brightly. 'Shall we go inside?'

Victoria had well considered that the place could be a shell inside, but at least she'd have been able to work with such an environment. Instead, the smell of damp and mould hit her nostrils as soon as they stepped into the once lavish entrance hall. She held her hand to her mouth as she gagged and waved at Kirstie, trying not to breathe in anything she shouldn't. Quick as a flash, her assistant produced dust masks for the three of them and they quickly donned them.

'Thank you, Kirstie,' she said absently, staring at the mess around her. Cobwebs hung from crumbling ceilings, the stairs clearly needed to be rebuilt as some steps had rotted away from the moisture eating at them, and the walls... Well, it had *some* at least.

'Are you sure we're in the right place?' Victoria asked as they hesitantly walked across the floorboards towards what she assumed had once been a drawing room. Or perhaps it had been a dining room? Maybe a library? There appeared to be a lot of wood in this room, some as panelling on the walls, some as shelves that had fallen from their brackets, pulling the plaster down with them. Rotted bookcases caught what little light was able to penetrate through the dust-covered windows that would look out onto the garden.

She focused hard, trying to picture the windows cleaned and bright, allowing sunlight to stream through as she sat on a window seat, a book in hand, and a spray of colour behind her from a garden filled with life.

'I thought there were pictures?' Cormac frowned as he stood in the middle of the room, turning in every direction trying to make head and tail of what he was seeing. 'Didn't we see internal pictures?'

Kirstie opened her phone and flicked through the emails. 'All the pictures are external,' she told them.

'But the pool, it looked freshly done?'

'Let me make a few calls.' Kirstie carefully made her way out of the house, leaving the two of them staring at the dilapidated décor.

'What do we do?' Victoria turned around to look at him helplessly. She didn't mean to moan or whinge, or even to turn to him for the answer every time they ran into a problem, but he always seemed to be the one to step in and save her. 'This was the first place I had actually liked. And outside is totally and utterly perfect!'

'It's okay,' he said, coming over to her and wrapping her in his arms. He held her close, rubbing her back as she burrowed as best she could into his embrace without dislodging her mask. 'So, we renovate it. Is it listed? Are we able to rip everything out and start fresh? Because, not going to lie, I'm not a fan of the derelict look the current owner is going for.'

She hiccupped a laugh. 'Me neither. I don't understand, though; it's like it hasn't been touched since it was built. It's insane.'

'Okay,' Kirstie said, coming back inside. 'Apparently, the external shots were taken in the early 1920s and colour was added to them digitally. Hence the gardens, courtyard, and pool looking immaculate. The place hasn't been inhabited since 1921 when the previous owners' grandparents died. It was sold in 1977 just before King Richard introduced the residency clause for property purchases from foreign nationals.'

'That explains a lot,' Victoria murmured before pulling herself from Cormac's embrace. 'Is it listed? Because I'm not sure we can keep anything in here.'

'Its listed for the exterior only. There was no access to the interior at the time of inspection and thus they only registered it for the aspect of viewing.'

'Well, there you go,' Cormac said, nudging her encouragingly. 'We can rip out everything and start fresh.'

Victoria nodded along to his words. She could certainly do that. Create the shell she'd been partly expecting. She turned back to the window, imagining her window seat again. They could have large folding shutters on either side.

'I don't want it all modern though,' Victoria told him. 'I'd like to incorporate some of the time frame into the house.

The seventeenth century and early eighteenth had a lot to offer; they used less wood, worked with more plaster and colour on the walls. Fabric was a big thing back then, too. I could get the royal decorators to help. I bet they'd *kill* for a chance to do something a bit different.'

'Well look at you,' Cormac said. While she couldn't see his grin hidden behind the mask, his eyes crinkled in the corners as they always did when he beamed that bright smile her way, sending her knees a little weak. 'A little interior design historian; who knew you had such talents?'

'*Pfft!*' She waved him off, but secretly she was overjoyed at his reaction. No one ever really saw anything about her; it was always Hattie being a prodigy, or Pippa's business success, or even Alexi with her dazzling beauty. But Cormac always seemed to find something to compliment her about, and it warmed her from top to bottom. 'It's just something you pick up going from palace to castle.' He rolled his eyes at her, but it was in fondness rather than derision or exasperation with her.

'Should we go and look at the rest of the place—or at least as much as we safely can?' he asked, holding out his hand. Victoria glanced from his outstretched palm up to his eyes that sparkled with happiness. Was he happy about the house? Or was it being with her? Was he thinking he could see himself here long term? Was he interested in more than friends with benefits?

She mentally shook herself before reaching out and taking his hand. He pulled her to him, wrapping his arm around her shoulder as they moved on to the next room.

She wouldn't let herself get her hopes up. No matter how good their sex life was, sex didn't equal love. But that didn't stop her from allowing herself just a moment of fantasy as Cormac began to paint a picture of a room, his hands moving in large arcs around him as he described what he thought they could do. She imagined him staying with her after she had a baby, running around after a toddler in the cosy room he was describing. But instead of staring at the floor looking for signs of woodworm, in her mind's eye he reached down to grab a happily gurgling child, just learning to take their first steps. He would pick them up and swing them around, causing the baby to squeal with delight—

'Victoria, are you okay?' Cormac's face came sharply into view as she jarred back, realising he was staring at her intently.

'Yes, fine.' She forced a smile to her lips, even though it was hidden. 'Sorry, I was just really into the whole... picture you were painting.'

'Yeah?' he asked, and she could hear the hopefulness in his tone. She nodded, and he turned away, going into even more detail of what he could see. Victoria cursed herself. She couldn't allow herself to get swept up into fantasies of *what ifs* and *might bes*. *She* was the one at risk of being hurt here, and she had to do everything in her power to ensure that it never came to pass.

CHAPTER THREE

*H*e stared down at the phone, typed *7-7-7*, and pressed send before tucking it away in his back jeans pocket.

'Yeah that looks good,' he shouted across to the guys who were sawing more wooden boards for the floors after peeking his head through the front door to the entrance hall.

After getting the house for the exact price Victoria had wanted—and a lot less than the American had hoped for—they'd ripped out all the internals; walls, floors, beams, absolutely *everything* had to be replaced due to the amount of rot inside the old house. Only the exterior walls were sound. The roof—the cause of so many of the issues—had to be taken apart and rebuilt, as had the grand staircase. They'd saved as many of the features as they could—the fireplaces for example had been fine due to their stonework—but there was still so much lost. Victoria had done exactly as she'd said and had managed to entice a few of the royal historians to come to the house and log everything they could in order to recreate the beautiful plasterwork that had decorated the ceilings and some of the walls. He'd never seen people so excited by such a task before.

After that, they'd thrown money at the project. It had to be finished before Christmas, no matter what. Victoria had stood there and told the project manager she didn't care about the cost, just get it done.

Cormac had remained tight lipped until they'd settled into the car where he'd opened his mouth, but she'd pre-empted him, telling him that if you wanted something done fast, you had to say such a thing and actually mean it. He'd wanted to argue, instead he'd closed his mouth and mused quietly on the way home, before finally asking if he could help manage the project a little more closely. She'd been delighted at the idea; her whole face lighting up before she'd reached over and dragged him to her for a kiss.

The two might have been a bit dishevelled when they'd arrived back at the hotel, but it was a memory that kept Cormac warm at night. Or day. Any time really, when he allowed the memory of her on top of him, her blouse unbuttoned and half down her arms, her skirt up around her hips as she rode him to ecstasy.

He was so lost in the moment, he didn't notice the stares at first as he walked around the side of the house. It wasn't until one of the workmen leaned out of the window from the second floor and wolf-whistled at him that he noticed something was amiss. He frowned up at the man as another worker pulled him back inside, laughing as they went.

'Oy-oy!' one man shouted across the courtyard. 'Aren't you a bit overdressed?'

Cormac looked up and saw the group of tradespeople standing around laughing and drinking, their t-shirts soaked with sweat as they pointed and nodded in his direction.

'At least now we all know why she married him,' he overhead one say to a newcomer as he held up his phone while motioning his head towards Cormac.

Cormac's scowl deepened as a deep chasm appeared in his stomach. Something wasn't right.

He dipped his hand in his back pocket for his phone again when it started to ring.

'What's going on, my Smurfette?'

'Haven't you seen?' Geri's voice was filled with horrified panic and Cormac knew that whatever she was about to tell him, the world already knew and he was once again three steps behind everyone else.

'You haven't, have you? Oh, my God, Cormac! I set you up with the alerts for a *reason!*'

'They were annoying,' he told her, trying to keep both the panic that was tripling his heart rate and irritation that she wasn't just telling him what was going on from his voice. 'What the hell have I missed now? Why are all the workmen being dicks?'

'Oh, God. Cormac, they're out.' When he didn't comment, having no idea what she was talking about she added, 'The pictures, from Monty's, they're *out!*'

'What?'

'The ones from the pre-season show; they're all over the internet and...' Geri trailed off for a moment and Cormac imagined her standing there, playing with her nose ring as she always did when she got nervous.

'Spit it out, Ger,' he demanded as he glared at the workmen who glanced at him, laughing and pointing.

'They've done a Photoshop.'

'Of?'

'You. And me.'

'What?'

'From the security cameras in the place. They took an image of me fluffing one of the guys and put your face on it.'

'Oh, dear God—'

For a moment, he thought he'd lost his hearing as the world rushed in around him. His sight went black, and he had to reach out and brace himself on a wall to stop from falling as the chasm in his stomach emptied into an eternal pit, falling endlessly through time and space. It was the one thing he'd *never* let anyone do to him; he didn't need an erection to look impressive in his G-string—or out of it. The other guys, usually the straight ones, all jumped at the chance to have Geri or one of the other girls help them out a bit before going on to dance. Nick had to be stopped using Geri's services because he couldn't keep himself contained once she got her hands on him. But Cormac had *never* done it.

'I gotta go,' he managed to choke out. 'I gotta get to Victoria.'

'Drive safely—don't get yourself killed over this.'

He pressed the end call button and shoved his phone back in his pocket. He took a few deep breaths to calm himself before standing and up and marching towards where his car was parked.

He heard the sniggering of the men as he walked past and stopped in front of the project manager who glanced at him with a wary eye. All his training with the royal advisors and Victoria's coaches had prepared him for this exact moment.

'Any of them discusses *anything* to do with what they're reading on their phones with each other or if they even *think* of speaking to someone outside of this contract about myself, Lady Victoria, either of our families, or the project itself will be done for breach of contract.' He made sure he said his words loudly. '*Cartwright, Daven, Mercer, and Associates* represent Lady Victoria and me, and I'm sure the King's own lawmakers would find it interesting to hear which companies are for and *against* the Crown.'

The manager's face paled, and the men near him began clearing their throats as they immediately found the plans or their tools far more interesting than anything Cormac was saying.

'Remember your deadline. I'd hate to find out you weren't able to make the date because your men weren't on task. I'm sure they'd all be devastated not to earn those big bonuses right before Christmas if there's even a *hint* of a delay.'

'Of course, sir!' the manager replied, nodding his head quickly. 'We're the best; that's why you hired us.'

'Yes, and it would only take a few words for that reputation to be destroyed.'

God, it's so easy to become one of them, he thought as he climbed into the large Land Rover Discovery. He'd sworn up and down that he'd never become the likes of Victoria's relatives, that he'd never look down on those who weren't as fortunate as he now was. He'd been there, he'd done that; he owned the whole wardrobe, not just the T-shirts. But at that moment, he knew it didn't matter where he came from; to those he'd left behind, to those that didn't know him, he was just part of the elite, part of the class that sat above them. And in their case, *way* above them.

He started the engine. Right now, *he* didn't matter. He'd known for some time that this could potentially happen. What he needed now was to protect Victoria.

VICTORIA HEARD HIM BEFORE SHE SAW HIM, HIS FEET STOMPING across the atrium floor as he marched towards her.

'Victoria!'

She sighed, putting her book to one side before turning around and facing a very red-faced James.

'James,' she said coolly, staring at him over the back of the couch. She was a little concerned by the look of sheer anger on his face, but he'd been finding it difficult to settle into his new school and every other day there seemed to be something else for him to complain about. Yesterday, the other children had apparently made fun of the way he'd asked for an ice lolly, calling it a lolly ice instead.

She braced herself for whatever travesty had befallen him today.

'Victoria,' he whimpered, his face crumpling as he burst into tears.

'Oh!' She jumped to her feet and hurried around to gather him in her arms. This certainly wasn't the usual reaction to one of his woes. 'James, what's happened?' The boy tried to speak, but Victoria had no idea what he was saying.

'Okay, hush now, it will be okay,' she said softly as she tried to soothe him. She held him close and brushed his hair back as he buried himself into her embrace. She glanced up at Toby who had taken to following his little charge up to the penthouse after a rough day. Usually, he could give her some clue as to what had occurred, but this time, their driver looked just as lost as she did.

'He wouldn't tell me anything, my lady,' Toby said quietly as he put James' things on the nearest chair. 'He either sat stone silent or sniffled a little.' That *was* concerning. Toby and James had been getting close during their long drives between the hotel and Highbourne and then back again. That James wouldn't tell Toby meant it was very serious.

'Thank you,' she said to the driver, who took that as his permission to leave with one last worried look at his charge. She carefully manoeuvred the two of them back to the couch, settling James in her lap before pressing the buzzer for Merryweather.

'Some hot chocolate,' she told the butler when he appeared a few seconds later. 'With extra cream and marshmallows. Mother's recipe.' When the man disappeared, she turned her attention back to James.

'Now, tell me what's upset you so much.' He sniffled, and Victoria forced herself not to react when he wiped his snotty nose across her chest. 'Did someone do something to you? Call you a name?'

He shook his head before glancing up at her with his big hazel eyes.

'They... they said mean things about Corrie,' he told her in an almost whisper. Her hand paused in its gentle motion of rubbing up and down his back and her brows raised in surprise. Why would kids go after his brother? It wasn't as if they'd done anything in the last couple of months to warrant them being in the news; their appeal had mostly died down after the wedding, save when they'd bought the house. But that had been a good thing; the locals in Earlshire were happy it was back in use and they'd had several property television shows try and get in on the renovation as it was such an extensive project. But other than that, they'd kept a rather low profile.

'What were they saying?' she questioned carefully. He sniffled again before heaving in a deep breath through his mucus-clogged nose and coughing. She gave him another moment to try and get his words together before she slowly pulled back and stared down at him. His watery eyes rose to meet hers, and she felt her heartbreak at the hurt and misery within his hazel orbs. She instantly wanted to gather him against her and cradle him close, never letting him go. She wanted to hurt whoever had caused such sorrow in this sweet innocent; who had the right to do such a thing?

Instead, she pasted on her practised face of concerned interest, biting back the fury she was feeling inside.

'Come on, tell me what was said and who said it so I can sort it out.' She held her breath as he made to speak, but the pinging of the lift distracted the boy. He sat up straight knowing it would probably be Cormac before he jumped from her lap as the second ping sounded. Victoria wouldn't admit, even to herself, that she felt a little disheartened that James left her embrace so quickly. However, she stood up from the couch and followed her young in-law to where he was bouncing from foot to foot, waiting for the final ping to announce his brother's arrival.

Cormac didn't even get out of the lift before James was charging towards him. Victoria heard an *Umph!* sound from her husband at the unexpected ball of hurt and suffering throwing itself at him.

'Hey, buddy,' she heard Cormac say. 'What's up?'

He stepped out of the lift with James hauled up against his chest, the boy's arms thrown around his neck and little face buried within. James said nothing, but a sob escaped him, and Cormac paused in his stride at the unexpected shudder James' body made as he began to cry again. Cormac's gaze instantly landed on her; his face twisted in surprise and confusion.

Victoria shrugged her shoulders and held up her hands in an *no idea* gesture.

'He said someone in school was being mean about *you*,' she confided quietly as Cormac tried to comfort his brother.

'Shit,' Cormac spat, far more heated than Victoria had expected, and the way his eyes shifted guiltily from hers made her hesitate for a second in her step to follow them to the sitting room.

'James, you need to stop crying,' she heard him say as she hung back in the doorway. She'd not yet felt comfortable in aiding Cormac in his parenting of his little brother, unsure he'd welcome it if she tried, but it seemed wrong to just turn around and walk away as if she didn't care. She did. Very much. Yet it also felt wrong to watch this moment between the two; James clearly still saw Victoria as an outsider, only willing to really use her when Cormac wasn't available.

She twisted her engagement ring on her finger as she watched her husband crouch down in front of the couch, trying to disentangle James from his bear hug grip on him.

She didn't mind James seeing her in such a way; she'd only known him a few months, but she really did want him to be able to see her as an equal to Cormac one day. But for now, she'd settle for watching and learning from her husband in how to parent.

'Dude, you know that I can't help you unless you look at me.' But James just buried in further. Tightening his little arms around his neck and trying to scoot off the couch and back into his brother's arms. The scene tugged at Victoria's heart and she wished she could somehow fix it. Or at least figure out what had happened.

'Do you want me to call the school? See if they know anything?' Cormac's hands paused in his struggle with James and she watched his shoulders sag as if defeated. It only caused more worry to twist inside her.

'Nah.' He shook his head as he reversed his actions and wrapped James in his arms again. 'I think I know what it was,' he confessed before burying his own head next to James' as if he suddenly wanted to hide away with James and disappear. Victoria couldn't help the feeling that it was *her* he wanted to hide away from. She gave him a moment to tell her exactly what it was before she finally sighed.

'Care to elaborate on that?'

'Check the internet.'

'The internet is a big place,' she told him as she walked into the room proper and grabbed her phone from the end-table. 'Where exactly should one be looking?'

'Oh, you'll see as soon as you open it.' She rolled her eyes at him before she pressed her finger against the fingerprint sensor and unlocked her phone. She opened the browser and immediately saw her news alerts filled with Cormac's face winking saucily at the camera or licking his lips seductively.

'What on earth...?' The words died on her lips as she caught sight of the headlines.

Latest "Member" of the Royal Family Revealed!
Newest Crown Jewels go on display.
Ooh! Pretty Whore-man.

Victoria sneered at the last one, but what did one expect from the *British* tabloids, she reasoned as she saw the name of the publication. She scrolled down the list of articles, all focused on Cormac, trying to find one with a little sensibility and truth in the headline. Not a single Avalonian news-site or blog was reporting it, she noticed, which didn't surprise her in the slightest. The King would have their media licenses revoked running such a thing about his family without first telling him—and he'd given her his personal assurance that this wouldn't get in the press.

She finally clicked on the much tamer BBC News article, knowing the old reliable broadcaster would report more facts than the sensationalism the rags would produce.

Cormac Blake, the newest member to join the Avalonian Royal Family has been revealed to have previously worked as an exotic dancer at a well-known male strip club in the country's capital city. Monty's *famously known for its Full Monty stripteases by men who are often described as Adonis' in their advertising, took the photographs in May to promote Mr Blake as their new rising star before he quit after Lady Victoria proposed to him.*

While the club reports that he was a firm favourite of both their male and female clientele, they admit that Mr Blake wasn't an employee for long, only starting at the club in January this year. However, other dancers at the club have said he was quick to learn the moves and really loved the attention it brought. When asked how they thought Lady Victoria viewed his work, they replied they weren't sure if the royal was even aware of Mr Blake's profession.

'It's not really something that you talk about,' said one anonymous employee. 'And you certainly don't want a new love interest to know right away. It's difficult for them to deal with... especially if you use the "additional services" that get provided.'

The second photo—while too graphic for us to show—does seem to suggest that sexual acts, to create an erection for the dancers before they appear on stage, constitute the "additional services" discussed.

The article went on, but Victoria stopped reading there. She kept rereading the words over and over—a*dditional services, create an erection.*

Victoria quickly pressed the back button on her phone and scrolled to where the worst tabloids were leading the *most read* section. She clicked on the very worst one, not for what would be a wildly outlandish and graphic story, but for the images the BBC said they couldn't print—she *knew* England's *The Herald* would have no such qualms of decency.

'I'm sorry,' Cormac said quietly at her gasp when her eyes saw the image of Cormac, shirtless, head thrown back in pleasure as *Geri* gave him a hand-job. 'But it's not me.'

Not him? How the hell wasn't it him? That was his face, that was his body, that was his—

No wait. Her heart hammered as she double clicked the picture and then zoomed in when she noticed something wrong with the image.

'That's not you,' she said flatly. Whoever that was had a tattoo. It looked like a snake twisting over the top of his shoulder and down his chest. Cormac didn't have anything like that. He'd barely had the money for food, never mind something so frivolous as body art! He'd also never had the chance to go through a wild phase with looking after James.

'The... *modelling* shots are,' he said quietly. Victoria stared at him sharply. But before she could question him, his eyes met hers then slid to down to James; he'd stopped crying now but still clung on tightly to his brother. She nodded slowly as she sucked her lower lip between her teeth as her mind began to race.

Okay, the sexual photographs weren't Cormac, but someone was claiming it was. They needed a way to mitigate the damage, to quickly soften the outrage that her fellow countrymen would feel and turn it against those who were trying to defame her husband. They couldn't say that the whole thing was a lie, they had to admit to some of the truth —the stripping—but they'd be able to use that to their own advantage. They could reveal Cormac's prior situation, it would add to the story they'd told the world. But first, she needed to know one thing.

'Did you ever use Geri for *additional services?*'

He shook his head. 'No, never.'

'You promise?' she asked, hating the hopeful lilt in her voice.

'Promise. I was offered and refused right away. It was to help boost *confidence* in those that needed it.'

Victoria couldn't help the twitch at the corner of her lips as the memory of Cormac's generous cock sprung to her mind. No, he certainly didn't need any sort of confidence boosting.

'Did she get paid specifically to do… *that?*'

'No, she was employed to do the accounts. Apparently, there used to be someone else, but she left, and they asked Geri if she would step up.' Victoria was surprised the young woman would engage in such a thing. 'She needed the job as much as I needed mine, so she reluctantly agreed. Why do you think she was so happy when Pippa offered her the chance to join her—'

'She's working for Pippa now?' Victoria winced at her

own voice. Even James turned slightly at her high pitch tone; he peeked at her with just one eye. Victoria cleared her throat before adding, 'Since when?'

'Since end of September.'

'Two months! I mean,' she said, lowering her voice again. 'Two months?'

'Ma'am, master James' hot chocolate,' Merryweather said from the doorway, holding a silver tray with the drink she'd requested.

'Thank you, Merryweather.' She walked to the windows to look out over the bay as the butler placed the drink on the end table. She had to start making plans quickly. She tapped her phone against her chin as her mind whirled with ideas; one of which would be easy to execute fairly quickly, she was sure Alexi would love to do it.

'You want some of this, buddy?' Cormac asked gently, trying to coax James from his hiding place against him. Victoria glanced over her shoulder to see the two of them now on the couch, James in Cormac's lap while her husband tried to get him to take a sip of the rich drink.

'Hmm? What was that?' Cormac coaxed, dropping his ear towards his brother's mouth. Victoria returned to her musings, allowing him to get to the bottom of however *this* could be linked with James' current state. 'I can't hear you, dude.'

'They said you were a *slut!* A *whore!*' James cried, jumping from his brother's lap and turning to stare at him accusingly. Victoria's head snapped around at the outburst, stunned that such language had come from such young lips.

'I looked up what those things mean!' he shouted.

'And what do those things mean?' Cormac said.

Victoria wondered how he could be so calm and composed as he asked his question before taking a sip of the hot chocolate in his hand.

'That you have lots of sex with women!'

'And'—he took another sip before putting the mug back on the table—'what does *that* mean?' Victoria stood perfectly still, holding her breath to see what James' answer would be.

'That you make *babies*! You make *lots* of babies!' The tears streamed down his quickly reddening face again, and Victoria was surprised at how much this was affecting the child. Why would Cormac having babies be so awful?

Oh! Was James going to feel this way when *they* had a baby? Was he going to resent Victoria for bringing a child—Cormac's *actual* son or daughter—into his life?

'James, I haven't made *any* babies. But why, pray tell, would the boys at the school saying that I make lots of babies upset you?'

Victoria had to admit, she was extremely impressed with her husband, how he remained cool and calm while facing an angry and distressed child. Victoria was torn between wanting to pick James up and hold him near or just run for it while she could, before she somehow got sucked into all this again. Although she was amazed that after living together as family for the past five months, she hadn't experienced this before.

'Because— Because…' James began to hiccup, his tears lessening as he tired to explain his young thoughts to his big brother. 'You won't be *my* dad, but you'll make babies with other women!' He finally screamed before turning and running from the room.

Cormac sat there, mouth open, eyes wide at the boy's declaration, staring at the space James had just occupied. Victoria, her mouth a perfect *oh* from her own surprise, stared between the stairs that James had disappeared up, the other Blake sibling, and back again, as she tried to work out what the hell had just gone on.

They both jumped at the slam of a door above them.

'What the hell am I supposed to do with that?' Cormac asked no one in particular as he ran his hands over his face. He glanced towards her. 'Victoria, I am so sorry. Those pictures—'

'Forget about the pictures,' she told him, rubbing at her own brow. 'I'll get that sorted tonight—'

'Seriously? What? Oh, I see, you'll go running to your grandfather and he'll click his fingers and make it all better?' he sneered, taking Victoria aback.

'No,' she snapped. '*I'll* sort it. Right now, you do *not* want the King here. I will sort it all out after we calm James down.'

And with that, she marched across the room and headed up towards the youngest Blake sibling.

∼

VICTORIA PAUSED AT THE DOOR TO JAMES' ROOM AND TOOK A deep breath before knocking. She gave the boy a chance to answer before she turned the handle and poked her head through the opening.

James had thrown himself across the middle of the bed, his head buried into the crook of his arm as he quietly sobbed out his despair and frustration at the world. Victoria braced herself; she'd dealt with this kind of thing before... except it had been the exact opposite. Hattie and Alexi had accused her of trying to replace their mother, while James was clearly desperate for someone to simply call a parent.

'James, sweetie,' she said softly as she stepped inside the room. 'Do you mind if I come in?'

He uttered something that she couldn't make out between the hiccuping sobs, his clothing and bedding, and what was probably a lot of snot.

'I didn't get that,' she told him as she stepped closer. 'You don't have to talk to me, and I won't tell you to stop crying, but I thought you might like a hug. I always feel a bit better after a hug. Do you want one?'

He shook his head against his arm, the hair at his crown flicking back and forth.

'Okay, well I'll just sit right here,' she told him as she took a seat at the head of the bed. She settled herself half propped up on the mountain of pillows that dominated the top of the soft mattress, ready for when he would undoubtedly come crawling over to her. She picked up her phone and sent a few messages to Alexi before she began to play a game that James had shown her a few days ago and with which she had become quickly obsessed.

She matched the brightly coloured gems together in rows and was soon lost in the addictive levels, trying repeatedly on an ultra-hard one. She bit her lip, her finger hovering over the *buy* button as she tried to decide if she wanted to buy extra moves or not. James had solemnly advised her that she shouldn't; they were a waste of money, something she was sure had come from Cormac when he supervised James on his tablet.

'Victoria?' James' whispered voice broke the quiet that had descended over the room. She lifted her eyes from her device and peered at the boy who glanced her way.

'Yes, James?'

'What happened when your mummy died?' he asked quietly, dropping his gaze to the bedspread where his fingers traced the light pattern woven through the cotton. Well, that certainly deserved her full attention. She put her phone down and considered him for a moment before finally speaking.

'That's a big question; can you be more specific?' He seemed to weigh up her words. His little face was so serious as he tried to work out exactly what he wanted to ask and how to word it. It was a good job she'd grown up with Hattie and Pippa, else the intelligence in the boy would have unnerved her.

'Did you get a new mummy?' She shook her head. 'Oh,' was his reply.

'My dad never remarried,' she said with a shrug. It was true; her father had never even dated again after his wife had died. No matter what her grandfather suggested, what her uncle outright said about him, or the public's uncertainty over what to believe, her father had been devoted to Princess Melinda and had been crushed by her death.

'Did you want a new mummy?' he asked shyly.

Victoria took in a deep breath as she considered his question. How would she have reacted if her father had remarried or even dated? She'd rarely thought about him doing either because he'd just never shown an interest. He'd always been busy with work, working all the hours he could, attending work functions, and going to dinner with clients or colleagues. Even his friends had been work contacts.

Victoria frowned at that thought. Had he done that because he'd been lonely? It had never entered Victoria's mind to think of him as lonely. If she had thought he was, would she have encouraged him to find someone?

'No, I didn't want another mother,' she finally admitted to James. His forehead scrunched up at her comment, and his lower lip protruded, quivering ever so slightly. 'But I was sixteen when my mother died. I was almost a grown-up, so I didn't need another mummy.' That made the boy look up at her again.

'But didn't you miss her?'

'Of course. With all my heart.' She recalled vividly the pain of her mother sitting her down and telling her that she'd been feeling unwell recently, that she'd gone to the doctor and they'd done some tests. Victoria had sat there with her heart in her mouth, knowing whatever she was about to say wasn't good. But when her mother had admitted the tests results said she had cancer, stage four, and that it had spread so much they didn't even know where to begin to treat it, Victoria had felt like her insides had just disappeared and there was a vast gaping hole within her.

'So why didn't you want another one?' he asked, sitting up. Victoria patted the spot next to her, and James crawled over and settled beside her, cuddling in with his head on her chest as she wrapped him in her arms.

'Because as I said, I was almost an adult and I still had my dad. Also, I had to take care of my sisters who were all younger than me.'

'Like Corrie takes care of me?'

'Exactly.' She gave him a little squeeze and allowed her words to sink in.

'Did… didn't Auntie Alexi want a new mummy?'

Victoria scoffed at the thought. 'When our mother first died, Auntie Alexi clung to me. She didn't understand what was happening and why Mother had had to leave us. She wanted *our* mum. And over time, she and Auntie Hattie saw me as trying to *replace* her. Auntie Hattie would get so angry at me, telling me I wasn't our mother and never would be.'

Victoria huffed a laugh at an old memory—upsetting back then but amusing now—of her sister throwing things at her to get her to leave the room. 'Auntie Alexie would just ignore me until I went away.'

She felt James sink in more against her, burying his head further down as if he was trying to hide from her words as she spoke.

'Hey, James, don't hide. Speak to me, tell me what's wrong. Why all this talk about mums, anyway?' It took a little shifting around, but she finally got him to sit up and look at her.

'I want a mum.' His words were honest and frank, and her

heart ached for him as his hazel eyes held hers. 'And a dad. I don't have them and everyone else does.'

'But you did—'

'But I don't *now!*' he shouted. 'And I never really did! Corrie tells me about them, but I don't know who they are! I never knew them! All I want is a mum and dad and that should be you and Corrie, but I don't know why Corrie won't be my dad! Everyone asks if he is and I have to say no and then tell them our parents are dead and then they make fun of me for having no parents!'

Victoria's mouth formed an *oh* at the revelation of James' pain and his confession that he wanted *her*, Victoria Blake, to be his mother. She blinked at the thought as he threw himself into her arms and clung tightly while she gazed, utterly surprised, at the door to the room.

'They weren't my mum and dad,' he sobbed against her as she pulled him close. 'They were Corrie's. I just come from them. Corrie's my dad, but he won't be my dad. And I want you to be my mum, but he won't let you! But he's making babies with other women and will be *their* dad! Why won't he be mine?' He kept crying and sobbing and Victoria cuddled him close, rubbing his back gently while making soothing sounds as she tried to figure out what to say.

'You know,' she started slowly when his sobs quietened a little. 'Lots of people call their dads by different names. Pops, papa, father, da; maybe your word for dad is just Corrie. He does everything a dad should, he just goes by Corrie.'

He didn't answer right away, but eventually his shoulders stopped shaking. Victoria said no more, just allowed him to calm himself down until, at last, he very quietly, spoke.

'But I want a *dad*. And I want him to stop telling me about *his* mum and dad, because I didn't get them. I just want *us* to be a family.'

Victoria made a sound of understanding and pressed a

kiss against his little head. She got it. When she'd first learned that Cormac didn't reference himself as *Dad* to James, despite his young age and having raised him from a newborn, she'd thought it weird and confusing, but had decided that if it worked for them, she wouldn't say anything. Even her sisters had thought it unorthodox—well, Hattie had thought it was bonkers. How could a six-year-old, even one as bright as James, process all that properly, she'd questioned.

Well now Victoria knew the truth; not very well, it would appear.

Mind, it had probably been fine until they'd got married and he suddenly realised that one day, Cormac could become an *actual* dad, and not just a Corrie.

'James,' she said softly. 'No matter what title you call Cormac or me, we *are* your family. One hundred percent.'

'But when you have a baby—'

'You'll be just as important to me!' she swore to him, feeling a fierce protectiveness over the boy she had never knew she could feel. 'I promise, you will be no less important in my life if I have a baby than you are to me now. I will still love you and take care of you, always and forever.'

He poked his little head up and viewed her with uncertain eyes. 'You love me?'

'Of course,' she said with a smile. 'How could I not love you?' He sat up before launching himself back at her, throwing his arms around her neck in utter joy. 'Alright, don't choke me,' she chuckled, unable to help the bubble of joyous laughter that slipped over her lips. James let her go, just enough to stare at her with eyes alight with happiness.

'I love you too! Can I call you Mum?' The question knocked the smile from her lips as she processed what he was asking.

'I— I don't think…' she trailed off as his smile slipped

away. 'I think that's something we *all* need to sit down with Cormac and discuss, yes?' James pulled away and turned around, crawling down the bed once again.

'Don't bother,' he grumbled. 'He'll only say no, again.'

'Again?' She sat up straight. 'You've asked him this before?'

He shook his head. 'I just remember coming home from school when I was little. We'd done families in class and my teacher said that really Corrie was my dad. When I told him he got so mad, and even though he tried not to show it, I could tell. And I know he spoke to Miss Derby because she wasn't very nice to me after that and always called Corrie *your brother* in a nasty way. So, I knew if I asked, the answer would just be *no*.'

'Well, that's not nice, on either of their parts,' Victoria told him as she made her own way down the mattress to sit beside him.

'How about *I* go and talk to Cormac?' She gently nudged him with her side, dropping her head over his so she could press a quick kiss into his hair. 'I could try and make him see it from a calmer point of view. Fewer emotions.'

James sighed, a huge heavy sigh as if he had the whole world on his shoulders. It was a sound that no child should be able to make and she briefly wondered how many of those sighs he'd heaved in the past.

'You can if you want, but there's no point. I think... Can I kill some zombies for a bit?'

Victoria glanced at the cupboard that hid the TV. It was supposed to be homework first, that was Cormac's rule. She narrowed her eyes before she stood up and marched to the TV cabinet. If she wanted a bigger role in James' life, then she was going to have to make some choices and not keep deferring to her husband.

She opened the cupboard doors, grabbed the remotes and

controllers, and chucked them on James' bed at his side. He stared at her with surprised eyes.

'Go get in your pyjamas and then go nuts. Kill some for me as well—I want at least *fifty* in my honour. I'll send Merryweather up with some snacks and a replacement hot chocolate.'

She winked as she strode out of the room with a purpose in her walk.

CHAPTER FOUR

♥

With a drink in his hand, Cormac stared out across the city towards Davenpool, watching another cruise-type ship pulling into the docks. It wasn't as large as the usual ones. In fact he wondered if it could even be described as a ship. It was probably an incredibly large yacht, but all the same, it was amazingly fancy. He supped at the bourbon and idly pondered if perhaps it belonged to one of those European billionaires. Apparently, they were becoming as crass as their American counterparts. Could be a Russian, he mused as he took another sip. The oligarchs often competed with the American super rich. Of course, it didn't matter if you were American, European, or Russian, they'd *all* love to get their hands on a slice of the Avalonian action.

'Cormac?' Victoria's voice called from the top of the stairs. He held up his glass to acknowledge her but didn't take his eyes away from the boat in the port.

Maybe they should buy one? He'd enjoyed their time on the royal yacht during their honeymoon. He reckoned James would enjoy the sea. They could sail for a year, see the world;

James would learn so much by experiencing different cultures first-hand. At least that way, he wouldn't have to deal with all the bullshit they dealt with here.

'Cormac, I managed to calm James down,' Victoria said as she came over to him. She glanced at the drink in his hand with a frown but didn't comment on it. 'It would appear that—'

She stopped mid-sentence and Cormac glanced her way. She bit her lip and stared out of the window; he could see the wheels of her mind turning as she tried to work out how to say whatever it was she'd come to say. She didn't have to; it was clear enough from what James had shouted at him as to what he wanted.

Dad.

It was a weird thought to be someone's *father*. Sure, he filled the parental role in James' life; he was his legal guardian after all, but he *wasn't* James' father. Their father was dead; how could he just assume such a role in James' life that wasn't his to take?

He wasn't a *dad.* He was a brother. An older brother. A *much* older brother. And he was only twenty-four, not thirty-eight or something more grown up, which you surely had to be to be a *dad*. He glanced at Victoria.

She was thirty-five. They'd had a lovely little party for her to celebrate the fact. She'd fulfilled the first part of the will's stipulations and now she needed a baby. He was going to have to become a dad at some point in the next five years.

He swallowed at the thought, before doing the exact same thing to the remaining liquor in his glass. He would be a father by the time he was thirty if they were able to have kids. The baby part of the clause hadn't really preyed on his mind since they'd signed the papers. Sure, they'd talked about it, but it was always *if* and *at some point*. And it wasn't as if Victoria was guaranteed to even get pregnant; it wasn't as if they could do anything other than have sex in order to even try and become parents, so he probably had time to get to grips with being a father in that sense, but James…

'I can't be his dad,' he said before taking another sip. 'I'm *not* his father. Our father is dead.'

'Yes, and *everyone* is very clear on that fact.' He didn't like the way she said that—what the hell did she mean? 'But James is *six*, Cormac. He never knew your parents—'

'I have done everything I could to ensure that he *knows* them!' He slammed the glass down on the nearby table, and turning away from Victoria, intent on leaving and disappearing for a few hours so he didn't have to have this conversation.

He *couldn't* have it.

'No, Cormac,' she said sternly, reaching out to him. It was the softest of touches on his arm, but it stopped him in his tracks. He swallowed, unable to turn and face her less he breakdown. 'He knows *of* them. He never *knew* them.'

'It's the same thing!' he protested. It was. It had to be.

'No, it isn't, Cormac. He knows what they were like for *you*. He knows how they treated *you*. He knows that your parents got to hold you and kiss you, tuck you in at night and tell you bedtime stories. That you went on holidays and days out together, that they saw you in school plays and waved you off on your first overnight stay… To him, they're *your* parents, not his.'

'But they *are* his!' They'd been so happy to have James. Surprised, yes. Hell yes, had they been surprised! But they'd been happy. He'd never seen his mother look so content as she got bigger and begun *nesting,* as his father had called it. She'd knitted all these tiny shoes and hats; she'd crocheted blankets and cardigans. Cormac had ensured he'd dressed James in everything she'd made and wrapped him up in her blankets. He still had them all tucked away in a box in their storage.

'What the hell do you know about all this anyway? It's not like *you* had to raise a baby and give up all your hopes and dreams when you were eighteen!'

He heard her take in a sharp breath.

'Don't you dare,' she said quietly. 'I lost my mother at sixteen.'

'And still had your father!' he sneered, spinning around again. 'You lot had your father to keep you together, you got to keep all of this'—he spread his hands wide indicating the luxury around them—'and your sisters got to go to university while you wined and dined your way through society—'

The slap echoed around the room. It was strange that it was the noise that registered before the pain bloomed across his face. He blinked, surprised more than anything else as he tried to process what the hell had just happened.

'Don't you *dare!*' Victoria said, taking his attention away from the sting of her fingers—oh they'd be talking about *that* later. The anger resonated from her as she glared at him, her shoulders hunched, her head dipped slightly; if she had super powers, they'd probably explode from her about now. His reset, the anger draining away, and everything became a bit more rational.

'Don't you dare belittle what I went through with my sisters! Different setting, yes, but the pain of losing our mother split our family apart!' she snarled. 'Our father didn't keep us together! Just like you, I was suddenly left in charge of running the house, making all the decisions, things I hadn't been taught to do!'

'Bet the servants helped.' He bit his lip as soon as he spoke the words, instantly regretting them. It was a thought spoken aloud, a hint of resentment he realised he'd been holding since they'd met, and he'd heard what little of her story she'd been willing to share.

She narrowed her eyes at him. 'They tried to take over. Half of them tried to brainwash *my* six-year-old sister with duty to the crown and all that bollocks.'

Cormac blinked, his brows raising in surprise at the swearing from her lips, and found himself staring, unable to comment, as she began to pace the way she always did when she was frustrated or nervous.

'The other half tried to swindle from the purse or tried to stop things Mummy had always done; it was why we had to move immediately *after* the mourning period ended. I was supposed to be mourning my mother, and instead, I was fighting staff and preparing for us to move because we couldn't trust them!

'And our father buried himself in his work. No matter what I did, I couldn't get him to come out of hiding. And to compensate, we got given anything we wanted, which sounds like a dream to everyone else, but it wasn't. It just showed how little he listened. I mean, he didn't even question when I said we had to move out and get a new place, he just said, *of course, I'll take care of it* and off we went!'

Cormac stepped back as her voice rose with every sentence she spoke.

'He bloody banished Hattie off to Guildford University two weeks after our mother died. *Two weeks!*' She turned to face him, holding up two fingers to him as if he needed further explanation, before turning them on herself as she added, 'And *I* had to be the one to pack her things because she flat out refused to, and Daddy would have just sent her there with nothing if I hadn't!

'I had to watch as Daddy forcefully escorted her to the car and threw her inside, and I just had to stand there and watch her go, helpless because I had a six-year-old sister clinging to me, completely lost, unable to understand *why* Mummy wasn't going to be coming home anymore, why her sister was leaving, and why she was being completely ignored by her father. And then she became a little cow whenever I tried to help her or tried to get her to do things, or told her not to do things all because she didn't want me replacing her mother because I wasn't *her*!' Victoria began to pace again, her hands moving through the air as she spoke.

'And then there was Pippa who just hid away day in day out, reading, working, studying. Trying in some way, shape, or form to beat Hattie so that Daddy would pay *her* some attention. She went from this bright, bubbly thing to this pale recluse and has been so serious and determined ever since. Meanwhile, *I* was only useful to my father by keeping Alexi out of his way, stopping her knocking on his office door, or immediately clinging to his leg when he emerged. That was until I was able to provide him some information after I'd been to Dottie's coming-out ball, a tiny titbit that gave him an advantage over his business competitors.

'After that, I became his favourite, not because of *who* I was but because of what I could become; *The Lady Snape*. So, I handed myself over to the wolves, took my mother's place, always telling myself it was to fulfil her legacy when in reality it was to try and get a smidgen of my father's love!' She shouted the last part as she stopped her pacing and turned to him.

She took a deep breath before adding in her regular tone, 'So yes, we might have had *all this*'—she held her arms out as he had—'but I'd have given it *all* up in a heartbeat to have had all that weight lifted from me and to have had my mother back! Alexi would have given it all up to have grown up with Mummy reading her bedtime stories, brushing her hair, and playing with her each day. Maybe Hattie wouldn't hate me so much if we could have had our mother there because *she'd* have been able to stop Daddy sending her away. And perhaps Pippa wouldn't have followed in our father's footsteps and made work her life if Mummy had found out about the cancer sooner.'

He stared at her speechless. He'd never heard her speak about her mother's death more than the facts and she'd always been so composed and together as she told him that she had stepped up to take on the mantle of *The Lady Snape*. She'd never made it sound as if she'd been through hell during the time. He'd just assumed that—

His mind faltered. What the hell *had* he assumed? That because she was poised, prim, and proper, she had no emotional turmoil underneath? That the death of her mother had been a cool and calm thing that had just happened and then they all went on with their lives?

No wonder the Royal Family still observed official mourning periods if *this* was the kind of life they led. Always perfect on the outside, an utter mess inside.

'I'm sorry,' he said when he finally found his voice again. She just shook her head and went to walk away from him, but he reached for her. His touch was firmer than hers had been; he didn't just want to stop her, he wanted her to face him as he spoke. She turned, but she refused to look at him.

'I really am, Victoria. I'm sorry you went through all that. That you had no one either. That you had to fight and take on something bigger than what I did—'

'It wasn't bigger,' she insisted, shaking her head and finally looking up at him again. Her beautiful caramel eyes shimmered with tears, and he just wanted to kiss them away. 'It was simply different. As you said, we had financial security.'

He nodded as he agreed. 'But, as you said, Alexi didn't want another mother. She wanted *her* mother.'

'Yes, but Alexi *had* our mother,' she reasoned. 'She didn't want me to replace her because I wasn't the woman who had kissed her sweetly of a night after she'd read to her or welcomed her downstairs every morning in a huge hug, whisking her up and spinning her around.'

A mournful smile spread across both their lips. Cormac imagined their own mother greeting them with so much love, and figured Victoria was thinking similarly.

'But for James, *you're* the only person who ever did that, Cormac. You *are* his father. And yes, *biologically* you aren't his dad, but right now he's a six-year-old boy who knows that the person who does all the things that his friends' dads do is *you*. *You're* the one who tucks him in of a night, scares away the monsters, and watches over him until he falls asleep. You're the one who has set up the Christmas tree each year'—he bit his lip to say they'd never been able to afford one—'and took him to see Santa, wrapped his presents, and sang carols with him. *You're* the one who held him when he was sick, who comforted him when he was sad. He's never known anyone else to do that and he never will.

'You, Cormac Blake, are everything you told him a dad is, and are the only experience he's ever going to get of one.'

'But... I'm not his father...'

'No, you're not his *father*, but you could be his *dad*. They don't have to be the same thing. Really, Cormac, you already are his dad in all but the name he calls you.' Victoria stepped towards him, her arms reaching around him, and he sighed as he accepted her touch, wrapping his own arms around her in kind. He pulled her close, her head resting on his chest as he pressed a kiss to her crown, breathing in the alluring scent she always seemed to carry.

'But I don't understand,' he admitted mournfully. 'Why does he suddenly want this now? Where did it come from?'

'He's just a boy, Cormac. He's probably wanted it for a long time; he's seen other children with their mums and dads and has probably questioned why he doesn't have them when you do the same job. He may be fed up of correcting people who mistake you for being his dad. Put yourself in his shoes, for just a moment. He's six now, but imagine having to correct people from when he was first told you weren't his dad, how old was that?'

Cormac groaned, pulling her tighter as he buried his head into her hair. James had been about three the one and only time he called him Daddy. Cormac had taken him to a park in the hope of meeting other people with kids, thinking he could perhaps talk to them and learn a thing or two about schools and what to expect as he grew out of the toddler phase.

There had been a couple of fathers with their little ones and James had pointed to him, calling him Daddy when the others had pointed out theirs. After their playtime, he'd explained to James again that he wasn't his daddy, but Corrie, his brother. James had nodded along and... Suddenly the picture in his mind was crystal clear, his little frown, a pouting lip, and then the little solemn nod.

I don't have a daddy, he had whispered and Cormac, not realising exactly what his brother was saying, had simply told him he'd had one, but he wasn't with them anymore.

'Oh *God*!' He threw his head back and stared at the ceiling as the enormity of what he'd done fell upon him. James hadn't been sad that their father was dead; he'd been sad that *Cormac* wasn't his father. Of course, a *three-year-old* wasn't going to understand emotionally, not even someone as bright as James! And for all these years, he'd been telling James over and over that he wasn't James' dad, that their dad was dead, and—

'Do you think that's why he was wetting the bed?' he asked as another thought dawned on him. James had only had two accidents since they'd moved into the penthouse, and neither of them had happened after he'd been introduced to his *aunts*. Was the bed wetting just anxiety of never having a family?

'Maybe.' Victoria didn't say anything more than that, but the way she shifted told him she still thought he was wrong not sending James to the psychologist like she'd suggested. If he had, perhaps all this would have come out sooner.

'I think you need to settle this with him though, Cormac, and you need to do it soon. Because if he thinks you've been off fathering children left and right with other women, what's he going to be like if—*when* I get pregnant?' He felt her head lift and he dropped his gaze back to meet her imploring eyes. 'He'll resent the baby so much, he'll hate that you'll be a dad to that child but not to him. That our child *will* call you Dad when he couldn't…'

He wiped his hand over his mouth, and the bristles from a couple of days of not shaving scratched at his skin. How had he been so blind? How hadn't he seen this before? Man, had he screwed up.

'I'm such a crap—'

'Don't you finish that sentence!' Victoria snapped, pushing him away a little so she could raise her finger to point at him. 'You've done an amazing job, and you've been on your own throughout. No one knows how to parent. Not when they first start out, and people say it's different for every child anyway!'

Cormac closed his mouth, considering the truth of what she'd said.

'You really think I've done okay with James? I mean, I lost our house and the little money that was left to us—'

Her hands on his cheeks, bringing his gaze back to hers, stopped the words in his mouth. She stared at him with a soft smile on her lips.

'Cormac, I believe those words with every fibre of my being.'

'I don't deserve you,' he whispered, his own fingers reaching up to gently stroke her cheek. 'I don't know what I did to have you come into my life'—he pressed a kiss to her lips—'I don't know what devil I made a deal with'—another kiss—'but I am so glad I have you.'

She smiled up at him, her eyes once more speaking volumes of her feelings for him, of her love and devotion that she had yet to realise herself. He'd promised he wouldn't say it, not until she knew it herself, but everything within him just burned for her to know. He took a breath and steadied his racing heart as he opened his mouth to finally speak the truth of his love for her.

'Victoria, I—

'My lady!' Merryweather's panicked voice called from the doorway. The two jumped apart and stared at the usually unflappable butler, looking rather flustered and distraught. Cormac's first thought was of James; had his brother done something in his misery?

'Yes, Merryweather?' Victoria asked before clearing her throat to bring it down a notch and trying again. 'What is the matter?

'I am so sorry to intrude, my lady, but *he's* here.'

'Who's here?'

'The King, my lady!'

∽

CORMAC HELD HIS BREATH AS HE HEARD THE THIRD PING FROM the lift a moment before the doors slid open.

'Where is she?' King Richard's voice echoed through the foyer and Cormac felt the wild tattoo of his heart against his chest. Would the King have him arrested for disservice to the

Crown? Would they be exiled? Sent to a foreign land, never to return? 'Where is that pain in my royal arse!'

'Richard, dear'—the Queen was here too?—'I keep telling you—'

'Don't tell me to calm down again, Katrine! I've had enough of all this! Balls to my blood pressure. It's these grandchildren of ours that will be the death of me, not my blood pressure!' Richard declared as he stepped into the doorway of the penthouse sitting room. Poor Merryweather danced behind him as he tried to get in front of His Majesty and announce his arrival. But as the monarch refused to give way, glaring across the room at Victoria, the butler gave up, cleared his throat, and began, 'His Royal—'

'Oh, don't bother,' Richard snapped as he strode into the room. 'She knows very well who I am.'

'Bet you get the finger wag,' Cormac whispered out of the side of his mouth before bending into his angular bow.

'You could be added to the scoreboard after this,' she replied as she dipped into the traditional deep curtsy that Cormac did not envy—the bow was bad enough if you didn't have a good core. 'Your Majesties—'

'Oh, don't you *Your Majesties* me, young lady!' Richard snarled as he began to pace the floor in front of them both. 'And get up; we haven't time for all the theatrics.'

Cormac glanced up from his bow, his brows raised sceptically, before he peered towards Victoria and reached out to steady her as she almost fell over in surprise at the declaration. She'd told him it was her grandfather who demanded such things and always ensured that tradition was put above everything else. Slowly the two of them rose, just as Queen Katrine took a seat and her husband stopped behind her to stare at them.

'Well,' he said abruptly. 'Would either of you care to tell me how in God's name those pictures appeared in the *British* tabloids? I mean, it's bad enough that there *are* pictures, but for them to appear over *there*... It beggars belief! Well, what do you have to say for yourselves?'

Victoria took a deep breath, and Cormac braced himself for another battle of wills between the pair. 'Not a lot,' she answered far more haughtily than Cormac thought was helpful right now. 'Although, I'd have to ask you the same.'

'What?' Richard spluttered. 'What on earth do you mean?'

'*You* were the one who said you'd ensure it didn't get out. And now there are pictures of Cormac and *fake* pictures of him all over the internet.'

'She's got you there,' the Queen said with a sniff as she looked back at her husband. 'I told you it wasn't going to work. I keep telling you, times are changing; the press isn't controllable anymore.'

'I don't control the press!' Richard's voice was filled with indignation. 'I'm not a *dictator*.' He glared at his wife as she pulled a face that Cormac could only describe as an *okay, dear* face. He'd seen it once or twice from Victoria.

'I am not!' he protested again. Katrine heaved a sigh.

'My darling, we know,' the Queen said, placating him. She leaned back and patted his arm gently with her hand. 'You have been exceptionally good to your people, but you have to stop treating this like it is still the 1950s; it's not. Good heavens, it's not even the 1980s.'

Cormac cast a glance at his wife and reached out to grasp her hand as she fought hard not to react to that comment. She'd confessed to him the whole scandal of her mother's elopement; of how she'd tried to jump the queue of marriage in the royal household, forcing the King to arrange the quickest royal wedding in Avalonian history for the Grand Duke, all to ensure the tradition was kept. Even if her mother had married a day before her brother. Not that the papers ever reported such a thing... Now he had confirmation as to why.

'I just give them a nudge every now and then,' the older man muttered, but he placed his own hand over the Queen's and gave it a squeeze before beginning to pace once again; Cormac wondered if that trait ran in the family. Not that he'd ask Victoria; she hated having anything in common with her mother's side. Save for her mother, of course.

'The story was leaked by someone in the royal household.'

Cormac's stomach plummeted, his heart sped up, and he wondered if it was possible to have a heart attack at the age of twenty-four. Did the King know he'd been in touch with O'Malley? That he'd been sending Marcus the pictures and texts from the wannabe gangster?

'You think it was one of my cousins?' Victoria shook her head. 'Even *they* wouldn't—'

'No, don't be silly,' Richard said dismissively. Cormac held his breath as he waited for the King to turn on him and announce to Victoria everything he'd done to betray her. Telling O'Malley about the night they'd met, agreeing to sell her out if she contacted him. Keeping secrets from her about the messages and working with her ex-fiancé behind her back... He should have just taken his chance when she'd proposed and told her. *Why* did he keep messing up every good thing that came his way?

'They wouldn't dream of it. Something like that; I'd have them packing before they could even think about saying sorry. No, no.' He shook his head and began to pace again. Definitely a family trait. 'They wouldn't risk their lives of luxury and ease for this. No, if it got out that they'd been providing the media with information on their own family, no one of worth anywhere in the *world* would touch them— I'd make sure of it and they know it.'

Cormac swallowed as the King continued to pace quietly,

mulling over the possibilities in his head. He loved a bit of theatre, according to Victoria. Was he building this up? Was he going to swing around in a second and point his finger at Cormac and declare him to be the traitor amongst them?

Cormac glanced towards the doors of the living room. He hadn't heard the lift coming up, but that didn't mean the Royal Guard couldn't come up through the staff entrance. A royal warrant would certainly override the hotel's security rules. Would they haul him out in handcuffs? March him across the lobby in a walk of shame for all to see, for the public to snap and share online?

'No, no,' Richard muttered. 'This is someone else, someone who works for us, I think.'

Victoria frowned and Cormac mirrored it, but for different reasons. He had no doubt she was trying to figure out who it could be, but he was flummoxed as to why Marcus hadn't shared his weak spot with the King. Would the Head of the Guard be in trouble despite working on resolving the issue quietly? Hadn't he thought it a priority?

A thought lit up Cormac's mind and immediately filled him with dread. He rocked on his feet as it hit him; was Marcus the leak? Had he been unwittingly feeding Marcus the information he wanted all this time? Did he want to hurt Victoria for not loving him the way he'd loved her?

He slid his arm around his wife and pulled her close to his side, needing to feel her against him, needing to protect her once more, just as he always would… If he could. She slipped her own arms around his waist, resting her head against him; so trusting, so naïve. It made his self-loathing swell. He wasn't worthy of such a woman, of her love or devotion to him, of the help she had offered him or her determination to make him her equal.

He didn't deserve any of this; no matter how much he loved her, no matter how much she loved him—even if she still didn't realise it. When they finally did manage to have a child and it came time for them to part as per their agreement, he'd tell her the truth. He couldn't live this lie forever, carrying this betrayal of her trust day after day. And if she did decide to follow up on the agreement and divorce him, he wouldn't take her money. He'd ensure James was sorted, that his education was provided for and that Cormac had enough to keep him safe, fed, and housed, but that would be all. He didn't want the twenty-five million crowns. He didn't need it.

He needed Victoria, his heart told him, as he held her closer still. But he didn't deserve her.

'But one of your employees wouldn't have access to the security footage to get the stills from the recordings.' The words slipped out without thought, but they were true and so glaringly obvious, he was surprised they'd overlooked it.

The stills had come from the club's security tapes and the only people who had access to them were Axel, Britney, and Sam who worked the security room. No one else was allowed in there... Although, he'd bet O'Malley and his goons were. And Harry.

Harry had been seeing Sam for a while, earlier this year; Cormac had walked past the room when the door had been ajar one night and had seen far more of the two than he'd ever wanted.

Dammit. Perhaps the security room wasn't as secure as it should have been. Maybe it really could be anyone.

King Richard stopped his pacing and turned back to the source of all his problems.

'No. We took the recordings. Marcus ensured every hard drive, every server, every *thing* they could have stored backups on were taken from that place you call a club and from all the homes of all who worked there.'

Cormac whistled. No wonder O'Malley was pissed off.

That stuff cost a fortune. He could well imagine his former co-workers being pissed at him too. 'Any one of them could have had a copy elsewhere and sold it on.'

'Not a chance,' Richard said, as Cormac voiced his opinion, starting his dizzying pacing once again. 'They were threatened with the Broken Hill if they didn't hand over everything they had.' Cormac shuddered at the thought of the notorious prison. 'We also ensured to replace their equipment with better than what they had to ensure no ill will against either you or the Crown.'

Well, okay, that would probably work for his colleagues, but it would still piss off—

Wait. Marcus had taken everything... Why wasn't the Guard here, with His Majesty? he wondered as he watched the monarch pacing.

'So, who do you think it was leaked by?' Cormac asked.

'If I knew that, I wouldn't be here!' Richard spat, turning on Cormac.

'Don't shout at him!' Victoria lifted her head slightly so she could glare at her grandfather. 'He's not in the wrong here.'

'*He's* the reason we're in this mess!' Richard argued back. 'If he'd had a job where he kept his clothes *on*, then none of this would be happening.'

'He did what he needed to survive!' Victoria shouted. 'I think we can all relate to that!' She narrowed her eyes at the monarch, who glared back at her.

'Is it true?' her grandmother asked, breaking the stand-off between the two as they slowly turned their attention to her.

'That I used to strip? Yes, Your Majesty,' Cormac said, ensuring his tone to the ageing queen-consort was respectful. He'd only met the elderly woman a couple of times, but she always seemed far nicer and much calmer than her husband. Victoria described her as the support her grandfather needed. She didn't foresee the Grand Duke having such a relationship with his wife once he took the throne.

'Tsk, child,' Katrine said with a dismissive wave of her hand. 'I know what you used to do; my husband tells me everything. And even if he didn't, I have my own people to keep me informed. I was referring to Victoria's comment—about some of the pictures being fake?'

'Yes, ma'am,' he said with a nod. He took a seat opposite Katrine and pulled Victoria down next to him. 'The posed ones are genuine; we took them for some promotional work for the show. And the ones from the security camera where I'm being oiled up before I go on stage are also real—some places are hard to reach.'

'Indeed,' she said, and Cormac swore the older lady had a little sparkle in her eyes, even if her face remained indifferent.

'The, err, racier ones,' he continued, hoping that clarified the matter without having to spell it out to the woman before him. 'Are *not* me.'

The Queen raised one perfectly shaped eyebrow at him. 'How can we be so sure?'

'Well, the body of the person they put my head on, has a tattoo on their chest and looks like it curls over the shoulder and down the back. It's just visible on the left side. I don't have any ink, ma'am.'

'I see.' And the woman's eyes dropped to his chest momentarily. If she asked to see proof, he was going to make a run for it.

'It's clearly not there on my promo shots and where the tattoo is, you'd have been able to see it on the other security pictures if I had it as well.'

'We need a plan,' Richard said as he began to pace again after listening to him. 'We need to—'

'Richard, will you *please* stop with the walking and join

us.' Katrine rolled her eyes as she spoke before heaving a heavy sigh. 'He's always doing this,' she told Cormac as she leaned towards him a little. 'I keep telling him it's not good for him.'

The King took a seat next to his wife, but the man didn't look comfortable. He sat perched on the edge of the sofa as he stared across at the two of them.

'I want a list of everyone you've had contact with—'

'Where's the Guard?' Victoria suddenly asked, sitting up straight as the thought suddenly occurred to her. 'Why isn't Marcus here taking part in all this?'

The monarch's eyes snapped to Cormac before darting back to his granddaughter at her question. *Did* he know about it all, about his deal with O'Malley, about the messages, the threats?

'He's off working on something related to this,' the older man finally answered. 'He's following a lead. Now, what I need you to do is ensure that you keep a diary of everyone you speak to and what you speak to them about. Use your clever phone or whatever they're called nowadays.' Cormac bit back the laugh that wanted to bubble up at the King's words.

'Smartphone,' Victoria corrected, pulling hers from her pocket.

'Smart arse,' Richard countered, and Cormac couldn't stop the splutter of laughter from him. Victoria cast her gaze his way, clearly unimpressed, before she began to do something on her phone. 'Same for you, lad,' the King directed at him.

'Will do, sire.'

'Also, we need to come up with a strategy to resolve these pictures—'

'Oh, I've already sorted it,' Victoria said breezily as she continued to tap on her phone's screen.

'Beg your pardon?'

'What?'

'Explain yourself!' Katrine, Cormac, and Richard all burst out at once.

'What?' Victoria asked, genuinely surprised that they were staring at her, stunned by her blasé attitude. 'If you had let me explain before you started on your tirade'—she looked at her grandfather—'I could have told you that I sent some pictures of us from our honeymoon to Alexi earlier and asked her to post them *immediately* to her social media. She quickly whizzed them up on her Instagram and they've already got three million likes.' She turned her phone around to show the group what she meant.

'There's three; it's a series,' Victoria said, sliding her finger to the right as she held the phone away from her, showing the selection she'd deemed acceptable to resolve the issue.

The first was the newlyweds smiling with glasses of champagne as the sun set behind them not long after they'd arrived on board. The second was a picture of the two of them fishing on the back of the yacht, their poles cast out into the ocean. They hadn't caught anything; they'd simply enjoyed spending time together and talking. But Cormac could see why she'd chosen that picture; he was topless in the shot and taken left side on—it was clear he had no ink where the faked picture showed it. A member of the crew had taken those first two photos and he wasn't sure exactly why it had garnered so many likes. His eyes dropped to the description in the bottom of the box.

My new brother-in-law is no prude as shown above; but that isn't him in those awful photos. Just check these out. No ink. His arms aren't that hairy, and he has a MUCH better body than the stooge in that crap photo does!

The gasp of the Queen and an exclamation of *what the!*

pulled Cormac's attention to what Victoria had revealed as the last of the photo series.

Cormac's eyes almost came out of his head as he saw the last image she'd sent to his youngest sister-in-law. It was Cormac *definitely* not being a prude. He was naked save for a black box that had been added over his cock. A rather long rectangle, which would have amused him if he wasn't so flabbergasted at seeing the image. He was lying on a sun lounger on their private deck, with the hint of the beautiful clear ocean on one side. It had been taken by Victoria on her own phone during their *private* time together. She'd snapped it just a moment before she dropped her towel and the two had made love; her straddling him and taking control.

His cock twitched at the memory, but there were more pressing things to attend to now.

He lifted his gaze from the phone to meet Victoria's. She stared back at him. Her cheeks flushed and her lips rolled between her teeth as she often did when she thought she may have upset him and was waiting for his response.

'And you were going to tell me about this when?' he asked.

'Um, after you had dealt with James and the whole... issue from earlier?' she replied slowly, carefully, not wanting to give anything away to her grandparents.

Cormac swore. He'd forgotten about James and the whole calling him Dad thing the moment Merryweather had announced the monarch was on his way up. This was just a testament to how crap he'd be as a father.

'I know it's not how you'd have done it, but it *is* working,' she told them empathetically, turning her focus back to the King and Queen. 'The likes are increasing drastically every second; look, it's hit *four* million just in the time we were speaking!' The three of them glanced down at the counter her manicured nail tapped at, to see it had indeed hit such a dizzying number and it was continuing to climb as they watched.

'What do the *hearts* mean?' Katrine asked curiously. Cormac realised the octogenarian probably had no idea about the whole social media thing and the likes of Instagram and Snapchat. Twitter would probably confuse her completely.

'It shows how many people agree with it—or just appreciate Cormac's body, Grammy,' Victoria told her with a giggle, which she quickly choked down as her grandfather scowled at her.

Cormac watched in fascinated horror, his eyes comically widening as the elderly woman leaned over and pressed her finger against the picture, right in the middle of Cormac's stomach. Victoria, similarly, stared at her grandmother, while her grandfather followed the line of her bony finger right up her arm to her face where she stared at the screen perplexed.

'Did I like it?' she asked, sitting back. Victoria and Cormac seemed to let out a collectively held breath as they relaxed their fingers. She hadn't, but Victoria told her she had.

'Good.' She sat back up straight as if nothing unusual had occurred, and she hadn't just rubbed her grandson-in-law's abs by proxy. Cormac was starting to like the Queen even more—he'd favoured her after he found out about the whole crown incident at the wedding. She seemed to have a bit of a naughty streak to her. He wondered what she'd be like if she had been born now with access to so much at her fingertips.

'Perhaps we need an application as such for the Royal House.' She turned to her husband. 'We could show the nation a little bit more about what we do. Keep them more switched on to us.'

'They're already switched on to us,' he countered without

even looking her way. 'So what? *That's* going to counteract the rumours, is it?'

'Well, it will certainly get people talking,' Victoria told him, turning the phone so she could see the screen again. 'Here are some of the comments...' She began to look through them, but the further she scrolled, the redder her cheeks went. Cormac did *not* want to see what she was reading. Good God, they were probably describing what they wanted to *do* with him. He'd enough of that when Geri sent him screen shots of the replies on her Twitter account when she'd shared a photo of the two of them having lunch one day.

'Yes, well, they're incredibly supportive,' she finally announced, quickly locking her phone and placing it face down in her lap.

'Well, whatever they say, it still doesn't tell us who the leak is. We have suspicions, which is *why* we need you to keep a tab of everything you say and to who you say it.'

'Of course,' Victoria agreed with a nod of her head. 'Right, Cormac?'

'Yes,' he said with his own distracted nod. There was one thing still bugging him. 'We need to find out who the guy was in the picture.'

'Beg pardon?' Victoria turned to him. 'You don't know who it is?'

He shook his head. 'No. We were supposed to be as clean as possible. Harry has a small tattoo on his right bicep. He covers it with an airbrush every night and has to do touch-ups in between. Joel had one over his stomach that he didn't cover, because it went just under the waist of his thong, so it was more tantalising to reveal it in full on stage... No one I know had anything like that. Even Ben's wings across his back didn't extend that far round, and they *covered* his back. Man, they were awesome!' he declared.

'So, it's an older picture; someone from before you started?' Victoria questioned, her eyes narrowing in thought. 'Maybe it was the person you replaced. Do you know who that was?'

He shook his head again. 'Nah, turnover could be pretty high, especially around holiday seasons as people came and went to visit family around the country. Harry might know. I reckon Geri *definitely* would. I'll give them a call later and I'll let Marcus know what they say.'

The King considered his words before nodding his assent. 'Yes, if we find the man, he can come forward and announce that it was him and absolve you of these transgressions.'

'What transgressions?' he asked before he thought. 'Even if it was me, anything *before* Victoria and I got together has nothing to do with us. Neither of us were blushing virgins,' he reminded the King. Richard's cheeks flushed with surprise, shocked at Cormac's comeback and the audacity of his words, no doubt.

'Not the time,' Victoria and her grandmother both said in unison. The two women glanced towards one another before turning to their respective husbands.

'It's a good idea though,' Victoria said, nodding at him encouragingly as she put her hand on his. 'But remember, people think we were dating longer than we actually were. So, it can at least stop people thinking you were cheating on me. I mean, even if it was supposedly during our breakup—I mean, you've seen *Friends,* right?' She chuckled to herself but stopped at the three blank stares aimed at her.

'Oh, watch a TV show every now and again!' she huffed before throwing herself back into the couch, arms over her chest as she pouted. Cormac couldn't help the hint of a smile that curled his lips; she looked adorable.

'Okay, so you'll find that out and report it to Marcus,'

Richard confirmed. 'You'll both report your conversations in a log and update Thomas daily—'

'Who's Thomas?' Cormac asked.

'His private secretary,' Victoria muttered.

'Cool. Like Kirstie.'

Victoria nodded.

'Yes, well,' Richard continued. 'Anything suspicious or anything you can think of report up to him or Marcus as well. Obviously, the more immediate the threat, go to Marcus.' The two of them nodded again.

'Right, now that we have dealt with the business side of things,' Katrine said, settling back in her seat more comfortably. 'Why don't we enjoy a spot of tea?'

∼

CORMAC MADE SURE HE SMILED AS HE PUSHED OPEN THE DOOR to James' room.

'Son of a *bitch*!' Cormac heard his six-year-old brother shout before a controller hit the wall right next to where he stood. Cormac jumped as it whizzed past his head and recoiled as it bounced off the plaster, nearly hitting him on the side of his face.

'James Ross Blake!' Cormac bellowed as he turned his furious gaze on his sibling, who stared back at him open-mouthed and eyes wide.

'I didn't mean to! I'm sorry; I won't do it again!' He reeled off in a hurry. 'It slipped and—' He stopped as soon as Cormac held up his hand. Cormac stayed stock still; he was fuming. This was exactly why he had always ensured that James played his games with someone in the room.

'No more games.' His tone brooked no room for arguments, and James knew this.

'For how long?' he asked, his voice little and small as he

raised his bowed head just enough to glance up at Cormac through his lashes. Little git knew exactly what he was doing.

'Until I say so. And,' he quickly added before James could ask the question of how long that actually was. 'Every time you ask me if you can go on it, or how long you have left, I'm going to keep adding time on.'

His brother huffed and crossed his arms, his pout extending even more.

'If you're not careful, they'll come and park a bus on that lip,' Cormac said as he came into the room and took a seat next to James. 'I thought I should come and talk to you after what happened earlier.'

'Did Victoria talk to you?' James raised his head and Cormac was beyond surprised by the look of sheer hope in his eyes. Victoria wasn't wrong about how much the kid wanted this, and Cormac cursed himself, wondering how much damage he'd done to his brother by simply not accepting a title of Dad all those years ago.

'We... talked, yes.' The hesitation in his voice must have made James think Cormac didn't know how to let him down. His eyes dropped from Cormac's and his lower lip trembled ever so slightly. His shoulder sagged, and he sighed.

'I see,' was all he managed to say.

'Just what exactly do you see?' Cormac asked.

'Nothing. I told her it wouldn't work.'

Well that surprised him. How much had the two spoken? To what depth? And why didn't he speak to Cormac in such a way anymore? He'd noticed over the last couple of months he wanted to hang out with people like *Auntie* Alexi and—

Oh. He'd never corrected James from referring to Victoria's sisters as Auntie. It was a title Cormac hadn't really connected to family; his parents had both been only children, and their parents the same. So, all his *aunts* and *uncles* had been family friends, people his folks had known for years and years. But to James…

James whose friends who had mums and dads *and* aunts and uncles… grandparents too. The image of James running downstairs and jumping into the lap of the King and calling him Grandpa made him want to laugh, but instead, Cormac cleared his throat and broke another promise to himself.

'James, do you really want to call me Dad?'

His little head shot up so fast, Cormac almost reached out to catch it. He nodded vigorously, that hope back in his hazel gaze. 'And Victoria Mum.'

Wait. What? That certainly hadn't been something Victoria had brought up.

'You want to call Victoria Mum?' Even to him, his voice sounded a little dazed.

'Well, you're married. And if your dad marries someone, then they're your mum.'

'Step-mum,' Cormac corrected absently. He paused for a moment as his brain tried to process that bombshell. As his mind caught up, he tried to push it out, to forget it for the moment so his brain didn't break altogether.

He felt guilty enough about what he was about to take away from their father, he didn't need to add his mother to his guilt-fest, especially on top of all the shame and regret he was hauling around regarding Victoria too. 'Let's just take this one step at a time.'

He rubbed his eyes that were suddenly tired. God, it had been a day and it wasn't even over yet. Victoria was currently downstairs having tea with the bloody King and Queen and she'd just asked them to stay for dinner—out of politeness, but they'd only gone and agreed! Hopefully, he'd be able to navigate *that* minefield.

What the hell had his life become? In less than six months, he'd gone from lowly stripper trying to hold on to a shitty little flat in the worst part of the city, to one of the richest men in the country having bloody dinner with the King and Queen! If his parents had been alive, the whole thing would probably give them a heart attack. He wondered what they'd think of what he was about to do, if they'd support him in his decision or hate him for stealing their baby from them? He prayed it was the former.

He sighed, dropping his hands to his thighs, before looking at James and asking, 'You know I'm not your *actual* dad, right?'

James' shoulders rose in another huge sigh. 'Yes, Corrie, I know,' he said, and Cormac was surprised by the sheer bitterness in his tone. He clearly expected Cormac to shoot him down again, to tell him that he was never going to be called Dad and he just had to suck it up and be more grown up about it. But as Victoria had reiterated time and time again during their earlier… debate, James wasn't a grown up, he was a little boy. And little boys needed daddies.

'But,' he began, and he saw James' body go still. 'I suppose I do fill the shoes of a dad for you, and if you wanted to call me Dad, then we could—'

'Oh! Thank you!' James cried, throwing himself at Cormac. 'Thank you, Corrie! Thank you!' He hugged Cormac so close, his little arms squeezing so tightly, while he repeated his gratitude over and over again, that it took a second for Cormac's own arms to hold him back.

'It's okay, buddy. And'—he took a deep breath—'I'm sorry that I upset you so much with this whole thing. I didn't know how important it was to you.'

'I just want a dad,' James whispered, and the words cut deep… pieces of Cormac's heart cracked, shattering in his chest, even though he knew it was physically impossible. Tears prickled his eyes and pulled James closer to him.

If they'd been raised as brothers, their relationship would

have been so different to what they had now. He'd have been off at university while James got to four, and he probably wouldn't have returned home afterwards, moving on to find a job, finding a girlfriend, one day becoming a husband and eventually a father himself. James would probably have felt more like a nephew than a brother to him with their age difference.

When he'd become James' legal guardian, they'd used that word so often, *guardian*, that the idea he was a parent hadn't even entered his mind. He'd clung to the word, always introducing himself as such and automatically correcting people when they called him James' father.

'Maybe,' he began, hoping his voice didn't betray the well of emotion that filled his very core. 'After a while of trying it, we can look at making it official.'

'What do you mean?' James asked, pulling back to look at his brother, surprise filling his tear-stained cheeks. Cormac brushed away the tears that still wound their way down his face.

'I mean, that maybe, one day, we'll look at changing me from your guardian to your dad officially, adopting you as my son.'

If he ever thought he'd seen James happy before in his short life, Cormac was wrong. Totally and utterly wrong. James' whole face lit up, his eyes brightening with sheer delight and elation at the suggestion.

'But we take it one step at a time, okay? When both you and *I* are ready for that.' James nodded enthusiastically. 'This is big step for me, James; I need you to give me time to come to terms with it.'

'I get it,' James said before throwing his arms around him again. 'Thank you. Thank you so much... *Dad*.'

This time, Cormac couldn't stop the tears forming as he held James closer still.

CHAPTER FIVE

'Okay, so we're all agreed,' Victoria said to Cormac and Kirstie as they looked at the calendar. 'The second of January is moving day.' She tapped the date on the large eighteen-month wall planner that Kirstie had been using since their wedding day to track their lives.

'Sucks we couldn't make it before Christmas,' Cormac said with a sigh as his eyes trailed to the end of the month. He wrapped his arm around her and pulled her close. 'I was hoping to have Christmas in our home and not in a hotel—no matter how fancy it is.'

He gazed down at her, his eyes filled with disappointment, and Victoria prayed she could keep up the charade and not give the game away.

'I know,' she said solemnly. 'But I think it's actually a fitting time for a moving in date—new year, new home!'

'I suppose,' he sighed. 'But, well, the decorating will all be done, why don't we just throw down an—'

'If you say air mattress one more time...' She playfully chastised him with a finger wag just like her grandfather. When he gave her a little smile, she pushed herself up on her tiptoes and pressed a kiss to his nose before falling back on her feet. 'Now, off you go if you're going to make your appointment on time. I'm so proud of you,' she added.

She beamed up at him, so happy that he'd finally settled on an institution to undertake his university studies. He was going to study law at the Stretton Guild University and Victoria was certain he would be as successful as he desired if his tutors' praise was anything to go on. She wholeheartedly supported his ambition to fight for those who had been in his previous position and had ensured she'd found him the best tutors in their fields for him to catch up and fill in any gaps he was missing since he'd left school.

They'd all praised him highly, impressed by how much he knew, and Victoria found herself both ecstatic and jealous at the revelation; overjoyed he'd be able to accomplish what he wanted and jealous that she'd never be as clever as him and her sisters in order to study something so important.

'I'm going, I'm going,' he said as he made to step away, making her frown before reaching out and grabbing his arm.

'Not without my kiss!' she told him.

'I don't know,' he replied, his voice dropping as he came back to stand before her. 'Do you deserve one?'

'Oh. Well, if you don't want to give me one...' She turned to step away when Cormac grabbed her and spun her back around.

'I don't think so, princess!' he declared before his lips claimed hers. The kiss was soft and sweet, and Victoria almost believed loving. She yearned for it to mean so much more than it did, to be more than a display for him to others. She sighed as their lips parted, her eyes still closed, clinging onto the hope that her wish would come true, that the man before her could one day return her feelings.

'I'll see you tonight,' Cormac said quietly, the back of his fingers whispering down her cheek in the gentlest of caresses. Another sigh slipped over her lips as she believed, for just one moment, he would be as eager to return to her, as she was to have him come back.

Her lashes fluttered open just in time to follow him from the room.

'Are we all set?' she asked Kirstie as the door closed behind him.

'Yes, my lady.' The papers rustled as Kirstie searched through for the information she wanted, having hidden it away in case Cormac happened to spy her top secret plan.

'The movers will ensure that everything starts to be delivered on the eighteenth—Friday. They'll meet you there at 9am sharp. I have told them not to be late.'

Victoria nodded, her mind racing with thoughts and ideas of how she was going to begin to set up the house. They'd been picking out furniture for their home since they'd first seen the building and she was so excited to finally see it all come together.

'Good, good. Cormac will drop James off at school that morning with it being the last day and I've arranged for him to meet a couple of the lecturers at the Guild for a tour and lunch, so he'll be busy until at least two. I ensured the Chancellor would receive a lovely donation in exchange for the favours.' She frowned at that, hating that she knew all the universities had been fighting over Cormac not for his knowledge and ability, but his ties to her family and the publicity he'd had recently, and what that could do to their popularity. She'd been happy when he'd chosen the small and quiet—but prestigious—Guild.

'Meanwhile, he'll think you'll be shopping in Earlsbury and will meet up with him at James' school to pick him up on time at 3pm. It should give you about four hours to begin directing the staff where you want things going. They'll then put that into play over the weekend.'

Victoria nodded. 'Very good. We'll then go our separate ways during the day on Monday and Tuesday to finalise our Christmas shopping,' she added as she mused over the plan they'd spoken about a couple of times. 'That way, I can head back daily and ensure it's all set for Wednesday night.'

'I have arranged for the staff to set up your meal before they leave that evening. They'll then return first thing in the morning to get breakfast ready, and welcome James.'

Victoria almost wanted to bounce with glee as she thought of Cormac's face when he realised they would indeed be in the house in time to celebrate Christmas—and for his birthday too.

'It's all perfect, Kirstie, thank you.' Victoria turned around to her private secretary and smiled at her. 'Honestly, I don't know what I'd do without you.'

'Thank you, ma'am.' Kirstie dipped her head slightly and lowering her eyes. 'But it's nothing; it's a privilege to be here.'

'Tosh!' Victoria said, before grabbing her jacket from where it hung. 'It's a privilege to have you. Now, I'm off to meet Pippa for a spot of lunch.'

'Lady Victoria,' Kirstie said. Victoria paused at the door and turned to look over her shoulder at the woman who suddenly appeared unsure of herself. Victoria frowned; Kirstie was a bastion of surety. She oozed confidence and never faltered. She was resolute, uncompromising, and unshakable, so seeing her have a moment of tentativeness in saying something gave Victoria a flutter of panic.

'Yes?'

'I was wrong,' she finally admitted. 'About you and Mr Blake.'

'Oh? Well…' Now it was Victoria's turn to pause. 'Thank you.'

Kirstie licked her lips, and Victoria knew she was preparing herself to go further. 'You both seem very happy together and you have obviously connected very well. I wouldn't have thought that when you told me of your, well, what I deemed *crazy* idea, you'd actually end up falling in love with him.'

Victoria stared agog at her assistant. How did she know Victoria's true feelings? She hadn't shared them with anyone. Not even her sisters. She was very sure to keep her feelings vague to those who knew the set-up, a possibility that something could develop, but certainly never revealing *I'm there and I wish he would love me back!*

Oh, God! Was she *that* transparent? Could everyone see how head over heels she was for the man she'd married? Did her sisters know? Was that why they kept asking how they were getting on? Did they want to know if she'd confessed her love and had her heart dashed to smithereens by her supposed Prince Charming?

'Don't worry,' Kirstie added quickly, probably seeing the panic-stricken look on her face. 'It's my job to know you better than you know yourself. To those in the know, they just assumed that you're happy and the arrangement is working. To everyone else, well'—Kirstie shrugged—'you're supposed to look that way.'

Victoria managed a nervous smile to the woman opposite her. Yes, she was supposed to know her very well, to anticipate her every move. To know what she wanted before she wanted it. But the idea that Kirstie could see her *feelings* unnerved Victoria slightly.

'I just...' Another hesitation. 'I just really hope it works out for you the way you want it to.' And with a firm nod, she knew Kirstie had said everything she was going to.

'Thank you, Kirstie,' Victoria finally replied, knowing full well her voice was far higher than it usually was. She cleared her throat, offered her assistant a shaky smile, and quickly opened the door. She hurried away from the truth that seemed to fill the room behind her.

∽

'Victoria, I want to take the mask off,' Cormac said, as he began to feel unsettled in the back of the car. As soon as they'd got in the Rolls Royce where Victoria sat waiting for him, she presented him with a blindfold and told him to put it on. He was not to take it off until they got to wherever it was they were going.

'No,' she protested, and he could hear the pout in her voice. 'It's got to be a surprise! It's your birthday present.' He had to admit that gave him a bit of a thrill; the idea of a present for his birthday, of actually celebrating it for the first time since his parents died filled him with a happiness he hadn't realised he'd been missing out on. Having a Christmas Eve birthday wasn't the best birthday to have, most people reported—the following day completely overshadowing it—but his parents had always ensured that Christmas Eve was all about him, and it seemed Victoria wanted to do the same. Granted it wasn't until tomorrow, but she'd told him she wanted him to herself tonight and tomorrow they'd celebrate it as a family with James.

But regardless of how exciting it had been, travelling for however long they had completely blindfolded wasn't his idea of fun.

'We've been driving for God knows how long now and I am fed up of the dark,' he countered. He heard her huff of breath and her muttering something but wasn't quite able to make it out. The soft sound of a button being depressed followed by the slow whirr of the curtains around them being drawn shut, meant she had activated the secrecy function in their compartment.

His interest was piqued.

Since they'd been together, she'd only activated the function a handful of times, always when she needed to speak to him, and that one time on the way back from the house... Could she be thinking of something like that again? While he was blindfolded?

'I could make it a little more fun?' she said breathlessly into his ear. He jumped at the unexpected touch as her hand slipped over his jeans-clad thigh. It seemed she was! 'I could keep you *very* entertained.'

'Oh yeah?' he replied, his own heart picking up speed as several ideas of what she might do popped into his mind. He licked his lips as she whispered *yes* into his ear. 'And how might you do that?'

He felt her shift in her seat, the sound of her seatbelt clicking open sent a shiver of anticipation down his spine. She leant against his arm, her breasts pushing up against his bicep as she pressed a kiss at the hinge of his jaw, right below his ear. He swore the whimper of need did *not* come from his lips.

If he thought the drive was long before she began her sensual torture, it felt like an eternity afterwards. She teased him over and over: a nip here, a bite there, a touch that promised more but failed to deliver, yet enticed him to yearn for it. When she'd finally kissed him properly, she'd straddled his lap, moving against him as if they were teenagers discovering how pleasurable the touch of another could be for the very first time. His hardened cock was agony trapped in its denim prison that she refused to release him from. And every time he thought he could take no more, she'd stop, and he'd beg her to continue.

He was about to rip off his blindfold and take control, finally getting what his body now demanded, when the car slowed to a stop.

'We're here,' she giggled, her fingers tracing over his straining cock. 'You might want to calm yourself before Toby knows what we were up to back here.'

'You cow,' he growled, but it only made her laugh heartily. He reached up to take the blindfold off, but her hand stopped it.

'No.' Her voice lost all amusement. 'You need to wait until we're out of the car.'

'Oh, c'mon, Victoria,' he sighed, but dropped his hand.

The door on Victoria's side opened first, and she told him to stay put as she climbed out and hurried to his side to help him out when Toby opened his door. He heard gravel shifting underfoot as he stood and walked the few steps Victoria led him. The door shut behind him and Toby bid them a goodnight before climbing back into the car and driving away, causing Cormac more confusion.

How were they going to get back to the hotel?

'He's not coming back?'

'James is in safe hands with Alexi,' she told him, as she positioned him exactly where she wanted. 'And we have all night to ourselves. Just the two of us'—she pulled at the ribbon behind his head that held the blindfold in place, and the softly padded material fell away from his eyes—'at home.'

He blinked, rapidly, as his eyes adjusted to the change in light. Although, there wasn't much of that to be had even without the blindfold, just a few lights shimmering through the windows of—

His brain stopped for a moment as his head darted from left to right as he took in the sight before him, and when it finally started again, the word Victoria had just uttered finally clicked into place. *Home.*

'But I thought we couldn't— Why are we—' He stopped trying to get his mouth to work and instead turned back to Victoria. She had a huge smile on her face, her eyes were bright with happiness and hope, and her hands were clasped and held to her chest as she waited nervously for his reaction. 'Victoria?'

'I moved us in!' she finally exclaimed with a small clap of her hands. 'Kirstie and I fibbed, we *could* move in before Christmas, I just wanted it to be a surprise!'

'Really?' he asked as he looked from her to the house.

'Yes.' She grabbed his hand and pulled him forward towards the entrance. 'And the best thing is we're all alone. No staff and no James…' Her lips curled up into a salacious smile.

'Are you wanting to christen a few rooms, princess?' He returned her grin with one of his own as his feet finally began to work. 'Wanted me all alone so you could have your wicked way with me in the pool or maybe on the snooker table?' Her tongue peeked out and ran over her lips, and with the way her eyes glazed over he assumed she was imagining the two of them entwined in both scenarios.

'Maybe,' she said, breathlessly. 'If we get the time. We only have tonight, and I definitely want you in our bed on our first night here.'

He threw his head back and laughed. 'You can have me any way you like, princess.' He wished she understood that he wasn't just talking about in the bedroom. He tugged her to a stop as she opened the door and was about to step through it.

'Ah-ah-ah,' he playfully chided before hauling her to him and scooping her up in his arms. She squealed in delight as he held her bridal-style and carried her over the threshold.

CHAPTER SIX

A wonderful feeling of deep peace and contentment washed over Cormac; he sighed happily and drew Victoria closer to him, her head against his chest, her leg thrown over his. Every so often, her smooth thigh would gently rub against his cock as she shifted. His overworked member kept trying to valiantly stir at the innocent attention, but after all the lovemaking they'd already done that night...

Heat spread across his face at the memories of their first time that evening and he made a little note to ensure he ran downstairs in the morning before the staff arrived and remove all traces of their sexual activities. He wasn't sure how Victoria would feel about the new staff cleaning up after their more intimate moments—he certainly didn't know how he'd be able to look them in the eye if they knew what he'd done to his wife on the dining table.

Cormac reached up and covered Victoria's hand with his own as her fingers played softly with the fine blond hairs on his chest. He occasionally waxed it still, undecided, after months of having to wax it for Monty's, if he preferred it smooth or natural. Victoria had taken to brushing and twirling the soft hairs whenever he grew them out, and he couldn't decide if it was endearing or annoying.

'I'm gonna wax again,' he muttered into the quiet. Victoria gave nothing more than a sleepy hum to say she'd heard him, neither agreeing nor disagreeing. He wished he knew if she preferred him with or without. Did she find the downy hairs weird? Was that why she touched them? Or did she find them manly? Did she think him less when he went smooth?

She heaved a sigh as she buried her head deeper into his embrace. It was almost a happy sigh, he thought as he lifted his head off the pillow to glance down at her. He longed to know what he needed to do to turn such a noise into a completely happy one. But what more could he do?

He'd been attending every class on etiquette and royal protocol she'd asked of him. He made sure he worked hard with his tutors, he'd kept the house on budget and *ahead* of schedule, and he'd even agreed to let James call him *Dad*. He'd ensured not to stand in her way of things, to not overly argue, and he'd done a photo shoot of the two of them in designer swimwear for an up-and-coming designer to help her get onto the pages of Avalonian Vogue, with an interview of him saying, yes he'd been a stripper, and no he wasn't ashamed; it had put food on the table, and a roof over his and James' head.

He'd also confirmed that he had used someone to help him oil up; sometimes women, sometimes the other dancers, and had flat-out denied that it was him in the racier picture. He'd told them that it was a still of two people who'd been in a relationship at the time and had since gone their separate ways. Yes, they could have been more discrete, but it was a shame that they'd had a private moment taken, twisted, and publicised to the world. Geri had called him up to scream at him for three days straight—she'd *never* been in a relationship with Enrico. She'd never stoop so low! He'd pointed out you couldn't even see her face in either of the pictures to know it was *her* and that it didn't matter if she had or not, saying they were in a relationship put a more positive spin on it... *legally* speaking. She'd shut up after that, knowing full well it could be spun as a form of prostitution under the country's laws.

The magazine had *ooh'd* and *ahh'd* over him, praising him for his bravery in going through the hardship of exotic dancing—he'd snorted when he'd read *that* description—and admitting to such a thing. They'd asked about Alexi's pictures and they'd been honest; the quicker they could prove it wasn't Cormac in the photos, the less chance of the media saying he'd had it removed or that it was airbrushed out in magazines, and so on.

The whole thing had gone far better than they'd hoped, even the King had grudgingly admitted to that. So, what would it take to make that sigh a happy one? A content one?

Maybe it was the baby or the lack thereof? But he couldn't help that, and it certainly wasn't for a want of trying. He smiled into the dim room at the thought of all the ways they'd been trying. She really liked the element of being caught; perhaps he'd take her into the gardens this week when the ground's keeper was out there doing his rounds and—

A noise, a faint sound of glass smashing somewhere outside the house caught Cormac's ears. His hand froze where it was on Victoria's back as his ears strained to hear anything.

There, another noise—not the same as before, but definitely not a normal house noise.

He pushed Victoria off him, climbing out of bed and tiptoeing towards the door.

'What—'

He shushed her, waving his hand behind him as he focused on the door in front. It was slightly ajar; they'd not closed it in their haste to get into the bedroom and quickly into the en-suite to rinse themselves of the mess all over them. He put his ear against the gap... Everything was eerily silent. Had he just been imagining things? Had it all been in his head?

Maybe it had just been security doing a walk of the grounds and they'd knocked something over outside?

He peered through the gap of the door into the corridor they were on. He couldn't see anyone coming towards them and there were no lights near the staircase. But would an intruder have lights? The staff weren't in the building, but they were still on site.

Perhaps a prowler wouldn't use a torch in case they were spotted from the guest lodges or the security gate?

Cormac cursed and turned back to Victoria who was sitting up and already on the phone. He made to say something to her, to tell her not to overreact, but paused. She'd lived with this kind of thing all her life. She'd told him about all the kidnapping attempts and the threats to her life—even the stalkers! Could this be one of those things now?

'Something isn't right, Marcus,' she whispered into the handset as she climbed out of bed, wrapping a robe around her. She hurried to the large bedroom window, keeping close to the drapes and peeking around as best she could so as not to be seen.

'No,' she whispered, before she dropped to the floor and quietly crawled beneath the windowpane to get to the other side to repeat her spying action. Cormac shook his head, unable to imagine what hell her life had been for her to remain so cool and calm in such situations. She was so aware of her surroundings and able to quickly think on her feet, weighing up her options and the plethora of outcomes from each. She didn't think herself clever, but he doubted *any* of her family could be the strategist she was.

'No,' she whispered again. She blinked as she listened to whatever instructions Marcus was conveying to her before she hung up without another word and threw the phone on the bed. She came over to him and leaned up to whisper in his ear.

'The phone went dead,' she told him, and Cormac bit back the swearword he wanted to breathe. They probably had a signal blocker. It meant they wouldn't be able to call security at the gate either, that was if they weren't compromised through betrayal or injury. He didn't know which of those options would be worse.

'We're on our own,' she added. 'Until he can get some guards here. He told me to head to the woods as quickly and discreetly as possible. Keep talking to a minimum. The closest asset to us would be Aunt Amelia in Stretton—if she's home. It'll take about twenty minutes for them to get here. I lost him before he could say, but no doubt he'll notify the police too. They'll be quicker.'

Cormac nodded, wondering how her voice didn't quiver and how her lips, when they pressed against his in a quick kiss, weren't dry; he felt like he'd drunk a cupful of sand; his heart raced as adrenaline coursed through his veins. The phone line dying could be a coincidence—reception wasn't great all the way out here after all.

Damn, he really wanted it to be simply that, but he had to assume it wasn't. That there was a real danger out there right now. And if they looked like fools afterwards, so be it. His job was to protect his family and right now that was Victoria—he was thankful James was still in Avon with Alexi.

'Put something dark on,' he whispered before turning back to peer through the door again. He still couldn't see anything, couldn't hear anything, and he considered where the noise could have come from.

O'Malley, his mind whispered, catching him off guard. Shit, was it him? Would O'Malley send someone after him like this? And if he did, how the hell did the bastard know where they were? *He* hadn't known where they'd be that night.

This is someone else, someone who works for us...

The King's words rang loud and clear in his ear as he heard the rustling of clothes from the dressing room as Victoria quickly changed.

He kept watch as he waited for her return, the same questions running over and over in his head. *Who's the leak? Do they work for O'Malley? Who else knew about Victoria's plans for us to move in early? Is it O'Malley's men coming for us? Will we* ever *be safe from the bastard? Why the hell didn't I tell Victoria the truth?*

'Who knew about tonight?' he asked as he took the dark jogging pants and black polo neck she held out for him. Victoria's face was bright white in the moonlight that filled the room, an eerie colour for her usually peachy skin and he wasn't completely sure if it was just from the moon or a reaction to the possibility they'd just stumbled on the source of the leak.

'I only told two people; Kirstie and Toby.' Her voice wavered, sounding suddenly uncertain, and that unsettled something deep within him. Victoria was never uncertain. She was always resolute, or at least that was the picture she painted. Even when matched against her grandfather, she stood tall and unflinching.

'You didn't report telling them to Thomas?' he asked as he bent down to tie his black running shoes.

'No?' His head shot up at the questioning way she said that single word. It was heavy with guilt, and her eyes focused on the floor rather than on him. He paused, not wanting to ask if she'd mentioned it to Marcus because he actually wanted her to give the same answer for the Guard; the doubts he'd had over the man he'd hoped to call a friend began to niggle at him again. And if it *was* the Guard, it meant he'd once more screwed up royally when life had given him something good.

Finally, unable to delay any longer save putting them at greater risk, he sighed as he donned the jumper.

'What about Marcus?' He pulled the neck of the top down just in time to see her bite her lip and look away. She shook her head. She knew she was in the wrong for not telling them of the change of plans; that she'd given someone a way to get them.

'Did you tell Alexi?' he asked.

'Yes,' she said quietly. 'But she wouldn't tell. I told her not to.'

He sighed. She should have told Thomas or Marcus —*especially* Marcus—but now wasn't the time to say so. 'Okay, so which one do you think is the leak?'

'Kirstie,' she whispered. She sounded pitiful, almost pathetic, but she uttered the name without hesitation. It wasn't the answer he was expecting. He didn't know either of them very well, preferring to drive himself and organise his own day. However, both had been with Victoria for years and it was hard to imagine that either would betray her.

But now wasn't the time to dwell.

He grabbed his phone, saw it also said *emergency calls only* and tucked it in his pocket. They might be able to get a signal when they got out of the house.

He turned back to the doorway, looking through it once more; no signs of anyone. He opened the door wider, thankful the old squeaking hinges had been replaced.

With his head in the hallway, he could hear... something.

He couldn't put his finger on what the noises were, but they weren't normal *house* sounds. Nevertheless, they sounded far away, perhaps on the other side of the manor. Were they the sound of *people* moving around?

But why would they be searching on the opposite side of their lavish estate? Kirstie had been in the house several times; she knew exactly where their bedroom was. Why would she tell them to come in from the far side of the house? Surely, they'd have come in as close to the newlyweds as they could. Hitting the sitting room would have been their ideal entrance. Had the intruders made a mistake or had Kirstie done it on purpose?

He glanced to Victoria and told her he thought they could make it.

'Down the stairs and to the front door. We'll be out in less than a minute if we go quickly,' he whispered. Victoria nodded and Cormac saw that change from devastation at their earlier revelation to focused and determined again, that steely resolve she had whenever she was facing anything down. He held out his hand to her.

'No talking from now.' Another nod of agreement as she slipped her hand into his.

He eased the door open fully and pulled her behind him as they made their way from one side of the hallway to the other, flattening themselves as much as possible against the wall. They stayed for a second as he listened again, his eyes adjusting to the darkness. The only light in the long, dark corridor came from the large window that adorned the staircase. The light it allowed lit the landing, making it impossible to see anything beyond save for a black rectangular void.

He cursed. They should have had cameras installed. Something they could have had transmitted to their phones, rather than relying on security. It was pointless thinking of that now, but they were being added. ASAP. No ifs or buts.

He slowly moved towards the stairs, his ears straining to hear anything out of place, anything that shouldn't be, but all was silent. The noises he'd heard before, the faint movements no longer tickled his ears. Now all he could hear was the deafening silence that made his heart pump faster in fear. He wished he could breathe quieter, that it didn't fill his ears, distracting him from hearing where potential dangers lay.

Victoria squeezed his hand, and he glanced back to her. She stared at him, the light from the stairway just allowing him to see her. Her eyes told him she had faith in him, believed that he was doing the right thing, that he'd keep her safe and get her out just as he'd said.

Cormac nodded, swallowed his fear, and he felt the quiet calm he'd always strived for before going into the ring in his teenage days. He could face this unseen opponent and defeat them.

He held up three fingers to her, wiggling his index finger to show her that they would go on the last one. She glanced at them before nodding her understanding and he turned back to the staircase, holding his hand up at his shoulder.

He took a deep breath. The first finger went down.

He couldn't hear anything. The second dropped.

It looked clear. The third one fell.

The two of them ran for it.

~

They made it halfway down one set of stairs, their steps light and quick as their silhouettes raced from one side of the small landing to the other before Cormac came to a sudden stop at the top of the next flight. Victoria ran into him, a soft *Umph!* knocked out of her lungs as she ran smack into his strong back.

'What—' Victoria began, her words immediately halting

in her mouth as her head peered around his form and saw what had stopped him in his tracks.

The front door was half open, allowing the silver light of the moon to steal the golden colour from the oak floor it slithered across. Whoever they were, they hadn't come in from somewhere else in the house. They'd walked in through the front door. Kirstie had given them the key.

He pushed Victoria further behind him, encouraging her to step back as he kept his eyes firmly on the space at the bottom of the stairs. She took the hint and turned, heading back across the short landing as he carefully took steps backwards, watching to see if anyone would appear at the bottom. But Victoria's gasp of shock made him glance her way.

She stood stock still, her hand on the giant knob that decorated the end of the banister and her face stared upwards. Cormac's eyes strayed from his wife up the stairs and he bit back his own huff of horrified breath as he caught sight of the shadowy figure standing at the top.

Cormac reached out and grabbed Victoria's hand from the wooden ball and pulled her to him. The man didn't move, and slowly, Cormac walked them back towards the lower flight, keeping his eyes affixed on the man at the top.

As he manoeuvred Victoria away, hoping to at least get her out of the door and away from danger as he took on the intruder, she gave another squeak of distress, making his heart plummet. He closed his eyes as he swallowed, before looking back down the stairs to see two other figures blocking their escape.

He'd been an idiot to even *think* they should have left the bedroom. If they'd stayed, they could have barricaded themselves in, locked the door, shoved furniture in the way. Opened a window to make it look like they'd gone through it while they hid in the dressing room, deep within the umpteen wardrobes it housed.

A hundred different scenarios fluttered through his mind in a second, and he suddenly questioned why Marcus had told them to run and not hide. Was the Guard actually part of it as he'd wondered? Cormac should have called the police himself. What if they weren't on their way? What if no one was coming for them?

That was what he had to believe. They were on their own and he had only one job to do. He had to get Victoria out of this mess safely.

He looked up to the man at the top and then back to the two at the bottom. The one at the top would be easier to foil. He glanced to the two at the bottom. One man alone—he hoped no others were hiding along the top landing in the shadows the moonlight couldn't reach—might be easier, but if Victoria went up, she'd be trapped. No, he had to get her past the two down there.

His eyes flickered between the three shadows. He was fine one-on-one. Even two-to-one he could handle—he'd learnt that after a couple of attempted muggings over the years—but the night at the palace had shown him that against three, he probably wouldn't make it. He swallowed at the thought, wondering what would happen to James. Victoria wasn't James' direct family, but she'd promised to take care of him, and Cormac was sure with her position and connection to the Royal Family, she'd sway the courts to ensure she got full custody of his little brother.

'You're not going to say anything?' one of the shadows at the bottom of the stairs asked. 'My, my, my, you were certainly chatty whenever you met Mr O'Malley—he sends his regards, by the way.'

Fuck, this really was his fault. He was the reason Victoria was living through another nightmare and why she was more than likely going to get hurt this time. He silently vowed he'd give his life to ensure that wouldn't happen.

He made to throw a comment back, but it was Victoria's outraged voice that answered O'Malley's messengers.

'O'Malley? Tell that bastard to go rot in hell!' she sneered down at them, moving back across the landing towards the duo at the bottom. She looked utterly beautiful; her long hair pulled back into a simple ponytail, she wore no makeup, and she was dressed in plain workout clothes, but in that moment, she was breath-taking. She stood before them as formidable as Boudica against the Romans or Queen Jane against the English. He'd never seen her so angry; she radiated fury as she glared down at the men beneath her.

'I have told that piece of shit a hundred times, he is *not* going to get one stubby, little finger of his on my father's empire. It is not for sale. At least not to *him*.'

So *that* had been what the bastard had been after all this time. Cormac had assumed O'Malley wanted to either sell stories on Victoria with the information he wanted Cormac to supply or to set her up for a public humiliation in some shape as a form of revenge. Clearly, Cormac wasn't as clever as he thought he was for not putting the pieces together sooner. After all, from what he understood, O'Malley's holdings were vast, but Patrick Snape's were bigger, better, and worth so much more than O'Malley could dream of. But a bit of insider knowledge, a way to blackmail the Snape family into selling it to him, or better yet, simply handing it over, would change all that.

'Forgive us, Lady Snape,' the same voice spoke up, and Cormac thought it sounded vaguely familiar. Was he one of O'Malley's goons he'd had the misfortune of meeting? He wasn't tall, like the one who got him in and out of the car, this guy looked shorter, nimbler. 'But it's not you we're here to see.'

'It's Blake, and what do you mean?' she asked, and Cormac could well imagine her face scrunched up in a frown. 'There's only myself and my husband here. And our staff,' she hastened to add.

'Lady *Blake*, my apologies. But, my lady, your staff are all tucked away in their cottages, away from here, your security... Well, perhaps you're best sticking with the Guard,' the man told her. 'But as I said, it's not you who needs to settle up with Mr O'Malley. *Mr* Blake here, has some unfinished business with my boss.'

Victoria's head snapped to Cormac; from the corner of his eye, he saw her face lit in the moonlight that came in above the window; it was marred with confusion and Cormac wished he could do something, say something, to make it go away. The weight of guilt that had sat heavily on his shoulders for five months, like Atlas had carried the world, felt ten times larger. This was when his sins would be revealed and the woman he loved would see him for the fool he really was. Naïvety explained his earlier failings; being green to the world of finance and adult decision-making was one thing, but making conscious choices to betray someone was completely different.

'And what business does my *husband* have with your boss?' she asked, not taking her eyes from him, and he still refused to meet her gaze. Instead, he kept his eyes switching from the solo man at the top of the stairs and the two shadows down at the bottom. Perhaps if Victoria kept them talking long enough to distract them, to let their guard down slightly, he could rush the two at the bottom. If he got the two on the ground fast enough, Victoria would be able to run over them, avoiding the one at the top.

If the third followed Victoria, well, she could run for miles on a treadmill, so he was sure she'd be able to outrun the third assailant. And if that did happen, he'd have a better chance of getting away from the two and catching up to her. Take out the third and then they just had to find somewhere safe to wait for either help to arrive—if it was indeed on its way—or for morning, when the staff would return and the security change-over happened, and Alexi would arrive. They'd be able to go straight to the King and tell him his Head Guard had been the traitor all along.

'As I said, my lady'—movement from the shadow that spoke caught Cormac's attention as he held something up—'the unfinished kind.'

'How'd you like to earn a little more than you're getting now?'

The colour drained from Cormac's face and he stepped forward as he heard O'Malley's voice clear as day ring out from the phone, or whatever it was the dick at the bottom of the stairs was holding.

'Good lad, you learn fast. I understand you have a few debts. Now you're listening.'

Victoria certainly was. Her head slowly turned away from him towards where the voice was coming from again, where the recording O'Malley had taken of their conversation was loud and clear.

'It's my understanding that someone is doing some background checks on you—'

'On me? Why?'

'Victoria—' he began, but she held up her hand to stop him, and he quickly shut his mouth. His heart raced for a different reason than just minutes ago. The bastards weren't here to hurt them physically. They weren't going to attack them, kidnap them, or anything else they'd been fearing. No, they were here to destroy *them*.

He was going to lose Victoria tonight, that was for sure, because after she heard this, she was going to demand he leave her. Those three words she already refused to say would shrivel up and die within her once she heard what they were about to relay, because O'Malley wasn't going to let them play the whole recording. She'd never hear how he initially turned the offer down. And no doubt O'Malley had a tape of his later call when reality had hit him, and he'd been desperate and scared.

'You rescued a member of the Royal Family and you're wondering why someone is checking on you? My sources tell me that pretty soon you're going to receive an invitation to meet Her Ladyship, and I want you to do just that.'

'Well, if she asks, of course I'd go. But I don't understand how this gets me more money.'

'All you have to do... is tell me exactly what Lady Victoria offers you. You do that and I'll clear all your debts and give you a nice little raise.'

'A raise?' He could hear so much hope in his own voice and it broke his own at heart how desperate he'd been, how close he'd been to losing everything...

'How about double what you get now, and I'll even give you fifty percent on top of your tips if... Well, I'll decide what earns you that when you tell me what she offers.'

'And that's all I have to do? Tell you what she offers me? What if she doesn't offer me anything? What if she meets me just to say thanks?'

'If that's all there is to it, that's all there is to it. I'll still clear your debts and give you the pay rise. A deal's a deal, after all.'

The recording stopped and Cormac slowly turned to face Victoria. His breathing suddenly shallow and difficult, as he wrestled with the realisation that his lies, his betrayal, had finally caught up with him, and now it was time to pay the price, and it was going to *hurt*.

'You're the leak?' Her eyes were wide in horror at the false revelation.

'What? No!' he exclaimed. 'Never! I wouldn't, Victoria, I wouldn't.' He stepped forward but stopped as she stepped back. She shook her head as she edged away from him, backing herself towards the upper flight again. Cormac's eyes glanced up towards the figure at the top who had been ominously still the whole time.

'You bastard,' she whispered, refocusing his attention on her, before shouting, 'You utter bastard! How could you!'

'I didn't, that's not the whole tape,' he told her truthfully. 'I declined the money; I told him no. I lost my job over it.'

'All true, my lady,' the voice called from below them. 'But I have another recording of his later call to my boss where he changed his mind.' Cormac's face twisted in a myriad of emotions; anger at himself and the prick downstairs, frustration that his lies were getting him deeper and deeper, and desperation that he just wanted Victoria to listen to *him*, not *them*.

'Is that true?' she asked. 'Did you?'

'Yes,' he spat out, his ire getting the better of him. He rubbed his forehead as she backed further from him, unused to being the target of any of his anger. But it wasn't her he was angry at; right now, he hated *himself*. But he had to get her to see, to believe him because he didn't want to lose her. He didn't want her to close off to him what he was so close to obtaining.

'So, you told him, about the proposal about—'

'No!' he quickly cut her off before *she* could reveal to the men around them what she'd really offered. He was certain that if O'Malley knew the whole truth, he'd have already sold the story, he'd have found a way to get the evidence and present it to the world and not only would that screw up their lives, have the world questioning their feelings for one another—potentially marring the nation's view of the Royal Family—it would make it so much more difficult for her sisters to marry for love. Instead, they'd be forever wondering if it was them or the money their chosen beau was really interested in.

'No, I told him *nothing*.' He bit his lip. Not exactly the truth. Sighing, he corrected himself. 'Okay, I told him that you came over to say thank you, that we went for lunch as a small token of appreciation and that James chose where we went. But only because,' he hurried to add when she opened her mouth to tell him that even that smidgen of insight was beyond the pale. 'We were photographed at The Meat Hut and it got into the press before I had the chance to quit Monty's.'

She lowered her head, and he wished she wouldn't hide from him, wished he could see her face more clearly. He also wished she'd come away from the flight of steps she was getting closer to, from where the lone guy stood above them. The way that one stood unmoving, staring down at the two of them, unnerved Cormac in a way that made his skin crawl. If anything else happened tonight, he knew it would be that guy he'd have the problem with.

'You lied to me,' she said quietly. 'This whole time, you've been lying to me, hiding things, running off and talking with Marcus...' She lifted her gaze, her eyes shimmering with unshed tears as she looked up at him through her lashes. The moonlight lit her face with that eerie glow again, washing out all colour, making her look otherworldly, ghostly. The thought sent an unpleasant shiver down his spine.

'Was Marcus involved?' Her voice cracked. 'Were you working together to do this to me?'

He shook his head, holding his hands out imploringly as he took a step towards her, hoping she'd let him. But she took another step back, backing herself up almost against the wall. He wanted to scream, to remind her to never put herself in a corner when there were attackers around. She knew this... He took a step back, ensuring she knew she wasn't trapped by him, that he wasn't here to hurt her in any way, shape, or form.

'O'Malley kept trying to blackmail me,' he told her. He kept messaging me. Marcus knew someone had to have given him my number as he was always messaging me. He asked me to alert him every time I got a message. He was trying to get to O'Malley—at least that's what he told me. I don't know if he had any other involvement.'

A scoffing noise came from his left, down the bottom of the stairs.

'Man, if O'Malley could get the Head of the Guard...' It was a different voice; younger, female, and one he knew *very* well.

'Britney?' Cormac's voice rose in disbelief at hearing the voice of his old manager from *Monty's*.

'Shit!'

'I told you to keep quiet!' the first voice snapped, turning to face Britney. 'Fucking hell, now we have to—'

A wail of a siren howling down the long driveway startled the lot, the two at the bottom looked at one another before shouting to the lone man to *run*! The duo turned in different directions and disappeared. Cormac moved to follow, before he caught movement from the top of the stairs.

The man who'd stood there hadn't disappeared back the way he'd come; instead, he bolted down towards Victoria, a flash of silver at his side. Cormac moved swiftly, slipping on the carpet as he pirouetted and lost his footing. He glanced between the man and Victoria, who had gone against her training, against everything Marcus had ingrained into her; she'd put herself in a corner.

He couldn't see her face but knew she would be terrified.

He cursed under his breath, knowing he'd lost the advantage with his tumble; he had no way to get to the guy and disarm him before he got to Victoria. Cormac had only one choice…

He ran, just a few steps, and threw himself in front of his wife, the woman he loved, the woman he would die for a hundred times over, just as the man thrust the knife upwards, and slammed the blade into Cormac.

~

Why doesn't it hurt more?

The thought floated through his mind as he stared back at the attacker. The other man's eyes, almost completely white in the moonlit landing, were wide in horror as he stared at Cormac—clearly, he hadn't planned on Cormac getting in the way.

A slurping-sucking sound filled the air a second before pain seared through his body. It ripped like fire from his gut all the way up his chest, to his head and right down to his toes. His fingers clenched, his stomach convulsed, his knees shook, and his head throbbed. He bit back the agonised cry he wanted to shout, to release some of the pain, but didn't want to give the bastard before him the satisfaction.

Cormac didn't see the man flee—he'd shut his eyes tight to fight off the pain—but he heard the hurried steps as the attacker disappeared.

It was not a moment too soon.

The strength from his left leg vanished and he fell to the ground.

'Cormac!' Victoria cried as she dropped to her knees at his side. 'Where did he get you?' she asked as she ran her hands over his chest, looking for a wound.

'Here.' He could hear the strain in his voice. He managed to raise his left hand, despite it feeling like it was made of lead, and laid it to rest above the inside of his left hip. He groaned, the pain intensifying as he pressed down and if he had been able to look, he'd have seen the horror in Victoria's eyes as he lifted his hand away and she saw it stained, his blood appearing black in the dim light.

She lifted his shirt and she gasped as the air hit his stomach and then it went silent, save for the wail of sirens that sounded so close now, yet still so far. A rustle of fabric tickled his ears, and Victoria almost whispered an apology into the darkness.

'I'm sorry. This is going to hurt.'

He didn't know what she meant, but—

He threw his head back, his neck stretching, the veins bulging along it as he roared with the agony that came from where she suddenly pressed against his wound.

'Cormac,' she said his name quietly, calling him back from the brink of unconsciousness, something his mind told him would help the pain go away, and he was very much for *that*. But her voice, her ragged plea for him to answer her, refocused him. He tipped his head up slightly, just enough to look at her.

She smiled at him, but it wasn't the one she usually reserved for him. This was a frightened grimace, one she was forcing out to try and comfort him, and he knew, the moment he saw it, that he wasn't going to survive this, that he was losing too much blood. He was becoming light-headed, and it was difficult to think, but he needed her to know. He couldn't go without telling her the truth…

'I'm sorry, princess,' he managed to say, his voice thready, barely more than a whisper, but he managed a smile for her as he reached out. She took his hand with her free one, pressing her lips to his palm before she pressed it to the side of her face, the closest he could get to holding her.

'I'm sorry, I never wanted to hurt you. I was an idiot, I was stupid, like always, but I need you to know…' His voice cracked and had a desperate desire to cough. It was becoming difficult to keep the breath in his lungs, but he had to tell her, she had to know…

'What?' she asked, searching his face.

She looked so scared he wanted to weep. He didn't want to leave her in this way, her hands scrabbling to save his life, yet completely in vain.

'Please…' He tried again. 'I love you, Victoria.'

Her eyes widened, her mouth dropped open and her hand, still holding his against her cheek fell, allowing his to drop to the floor with a thud. It was strange, he barely felt it.

'I love you, Victoria, with all my heart and being.' He smiled softly at her and a sob bubbled up over her lips. 'Don't cry, princess. Don't cry…'

'No, Cormac, no!' She was pleading, but her voice gained volume and strength. She shifted, applying more pressure on his stomach, so much lighter than he really knew it must be. 'You fight!' she ordered him. 'You bloody well hold on! Don't leave me! Don't you dare leave me!' she cried.

'Ah, princess, I am sorry.'

'No,' she protested. 'Don't. Don't, please.' He wished she wouldn't cry or that his arm would work so he could brush her tears away. 'You can't, please, don't you understand, you can't. Not now. Please. Please.'

He smiled at her, his gently lopsided smile that he saved just for her during their more tender moments. At least he hoped he did. His brain was telling him again that it would be better if he slept. That if he just closed his eyes, all would be better when he woke up.

'I love you too, Cormac Blake.'

Her words were quiet; they sounded so far away, but he held them close, tucked them safely inside his heart as he felt the warm arms of the Sandman wrap themselves around him…

KEEPING HIM

∼

'I LOVE YOU TOO, CORMAC BLAKE. PLEASE,' SHE BEGGED AS HIS eyes fluttered closed and his head lolled to one side. 'Please hold on, please! Somebody!' She shouted into the empty house. 'Someone—anyone!—help us! Help him!' Her voice cracked, huge wracking sobs spilled from her lips as she pressed her top against his wound harder as blood that appeared as black as ink in the dim light, began to seep from under where the fabric sat.

Too quick, she thought as she stared at the staining of his chalk white skin—she hoped his complexion was from the moonlight that slivered through the window above them and not from lack of blood.

The sirens were louder, so close, but they were the police, the Guard, they weren't the paramedics, and her husband was going to bleed out before they'd be able to get medical assistance here.

Cormac was going to die.

Right here. Right now.

In her arms.

'No,' she snarled, anger replacing the clawing panic inside her. 'No! Don't you dare, Cormac Blake! Don't you *fucking dare leave me*!'

'Victoria?' Marcus' voice called up the stairs as the sounds tires skidded to a halt on the gravel driveway beyond the still open door. 'Victoria where are you?'

'Here!' she cried back, a sprig of hope blooming in her chest. 'The landing. Oh, Marcus, help!'

She applied more pressure to Cormac's wound, hissing at him to *stay with her*, praying that he'd survive that he'd—

'Come away, Victoria.' Marcus heaved her up, dragging her away from her beloved, and she screamed, clawing at his hands, kicking at the air, as he spun her around.

'No! I have to keep pressure on it! He has to live!'

'Then let them work,' his deep voice told her as her feet once against touched the ground, but his arms stayed wrapped around her waist, holding her close so she couldn't run and interfere.

Paramedics surrounded her husband; bags filled with medical supplies and equipment meant to save lives, at their side.

'They're here, Cormac!' she called to him, hoping he heard her. 'You damn well hold on! Because they're here!"

'They'll do their best,' Marcus murmured as someone set up a bright, emergency lamp over the crew.

Oh no, they better do damn well better than that! Victoria's brain screamed.

'You better save him!' she shouted at the medical team. 'You better save him or you'll face the king directly to explain why you didn't! Why you let a member of the Royal Family die! You'll be straight to the Hill if you—'

'That's enough,' Marcus told her, forcibly turning her, shaking her until she gazed up at him. 'They'll do everything they can, but you're not helping them with this... tirade.'

'He has to live,' she whispered.

The sympathy, a belief that it was already too late to save the man she loved, shimmering in Marcus' deep, dark eyes, only riled her up further. She fought him off, shaking away his grip on her shoulders and faced the medical team again.

'If you don't save him, I'll personally see you ruined,' she sneered. 'And you, Cormac Dean Blake, if you don't pull through, I'll take it all back! I will! I'll take'—she hiccuped on an unexpected sob—'back. I'll stop- stop loving you! I'll take it back... I'll stop... I'll...'

Marcus' arms caught her just before she collapsed into a heap of tears...

CHAPTER SEVEN

The tea was horrid. A pale, milky colour that seemed to sit under a rim of clear water. The string of the tea bag ran up the side of the polystyrene cup, giving Victoria something to play with as she sat and waited.

It was so quiet, *too* quiet in the small hospital of Earlsbury. It was the nearest one to them, and they were lucky it had an emergency department *and* the facilities to treat Cormac, but she wished they were in Avon, in the great, glistening citadel of the pristine Royal Infirmary with the royal physicians up in the royal suite. At least in the capital, the hospital would be bustling with activity as people came and went and she'd be able to distract herself by watching them, maybe talking to someone who was in the same situation. They'd be able to cling to one another, keep each other from constantly thinking about what would happen if—

She threw the cup across the narrow hallway. The tea sprayed up the off-white walls, a pale tan colour that barely made a difference to the paint. The polystyrene harmlessly bounced off the wall to the floor, rolling in small circles until it slowed and swayed to a stop.

She growled, holding her face in her hands, wanting to pull the skin from her bones as she bit back the howl of frustration threatening to rip through her. She couldn't even have the satisfaction of breaking something to help calm the restless feeling that raced under her skin. She wanted to march through the hallways and demand to know what was happening, to stand in the operating theatre and watch the doctors, ordering them not to stop, that they *make* Cormac survive.

I love you, Victoria, with all my heart and being.

She rested her head against the wall behind her as she fought the tears that wanted to fall. He loved her. He loved her with all his heart, all his being. That wasn't just something a dying man said, was it? He wouldn't say that just because he thought he wasn't going to make it, would he? Cormac wasn't religious, but he wouldn't say something like if he didn't mean it and knew the lie would be forever in the world. He wasn't a liar—

But he was. That was why those people had been at the house, why they'd been attacked, why Cormac was now lying on a hospital bed, doctors poking around inside him as he fought for his life.

He'd betrayed her before he even knew her.

Before he loved her.

If he loved her at all, and it wasn't just another lie in case he pulled through and wanted to remain in her good books.

She let another frustrated growl out, jamming her hands under her legs to stop them from scratching at her skin, and kicked her feet out fruitlessly to just get rid of some of the anger that coursed through her.

How had she been so blind? He'd let her think that Kirstie or Toby was the leak, when really it was him and—

The heavenly, deep scent of Assam tea filled her nose; she breathed in deeply and felt her whole body sway as all the worry, all the frustration, the adrenaline that had been keeping her going, drained from her and she leaned forward into the aroma.

'Thought this might be what you need,' Marcus' familiar deep voice made her jump. She opened her eyes and saw a beautiful china cup filled with a brew the perfect colour—a bright, vibrant, burnt orange—before her. She swallowed, wishing she could take it, but she kept her hands placed firmly under her thighs as she glanced up from the tea to her ex.

His brows were lowered over his almost black eyes as he stared down at her, unsure why she wasn't taking the proffered cup.

'It's your own tea—I promise.'

That only made her frown harder.

'And why,' she asked through gritted teeth. 'Do *you* have my preferred tea here?'

The man sighed, taking the cup back into his own hands as he took a seat next to her. The delicate white porcelain looked ridiculous in his large hands as he cradled it gently.

'We caught almost all of them,' he told her. 'Two managed to escape from what I can tell. We caught four coming out of the house, but apparently there were six in the property—'

'We only ran into three of them.'

'They had the others covering all the potential exits just in case you didn't go for the most obvious and easiest of routes. And just in case you decided to climb out of the window, there were another five positioned outside.'

That raised her brows. Eleven. Quite a number to deliver *just* a message.

'And how many stood amongst the Guard?'

Marcus narrowed his gaze at her. 'What's that supposed to mean?'

'We have a history, Marcus; if you *ever* cared for me, you'll answer this truthfully. Are you part of the leak?'

'Fuck off, Victoria.'

She startled at his crude language. He'd never once, in all their time together, even in their most intimate moments, ever spoken such words. For the first few months of their time as a couple, she'd wondered if they were even in his vocabulary, until she happened upon him talking to some other Guards, telling lewd jokes, and joining in with their revelry. She'd tried to get him to say colourful things to her in the bedroom, to say what he was going to do to her in such debauched language, but he never had.

A sudden dawning realization hit her out of the blue; she had never really been in love with the man before her if her feelings for Cormac were indeed what love was.

Yes, she had loved Marcus, he had been safe and warm. He'd been *nice*, a friend and a confidant when she'd been so desperate for such a person in her life.

But she'd never been *in* love with him...

She began to laugh. A stupid, inappropriate giggle bubbled its way up her throat. She tried to stop it, tried to bite it down, but it burst out of her, a wild bark of laughter that slipped from her lips, shaking her shoulders as it took her in earnest.

'Victoria?' Marcus' concerned voice caught her ear, but it only made her laugh harder. Good God, she'd been an idiot. For years she'd pined over a man that she'd never actually been totally and completely in love with. She'd been holding a grudge against him simply because her *pride*, not her heart, had been hurt. She'd avoided him as much as she could and sent him snide looks, made cutting remarks, and ensured he knew she was his superior when she couldn't.

Even now, she was trying to find a way for him to be at fault, that he was trying to hurt her once more, when really all he'd ever done was to look out for her. Even now, sitting in hospital miles from home, he'd brought her the one thing she turned to when things got tough. A cup of her favourite tea.

He'd been trying to be her friend and she'd been the one refusing such an offer. She was almost as big an idiot as Cormac had been!

'Oh, God, Marcus,' she breathed as she finally managed to get her giggles under control. 'Marcus, I am sorry, I am so, so sorry...' And suddenly the laughter became tears. Great, racking sobs she couldn't control.

'Bloody hell!' The tinkling of the teacup being set down somewhere gave her just enough notice that he was about to pull her into his arms, and she went willingly, burying herself against him.

The tears fell as she tried to explain to him how she'd suspected him and how that made her feel. Tried to tell him her fears of everything she'd have to face if Cormac didn't make it, and how would she be able to face him if he did.

But the tears wouldn't stop, and she knew that he had no idea what she was really saying, but rather than shush her, he just allowed her to carry on, to get everything off her chest, to have her moment before she began to pull herself back together so she could face the whole thing head on.

'So, want to try that again?' Marcus asked as she pulled herself out of his embrace and wiped away the tears. She huffed a laugh, a real one this time, even if it was only small.

'Cormac was working for Conner O'Malley all this time,' she said quietly, tucking her bedraggled hair behind her ears and dropping her eyes to the floor. 'They had this tape of him agreeing to tell O'Malley about what I was going to offer him.'

'I know,' he said, as he leaned away, reaching down to get something. 'He confessed it all to me before the wedding.'

'The wedding!' Her voice went high and screechy, causing Marcus to look at her pointedly as he sat back up, delicate teacup in his fingers once more.

'Yes, Victoria, the wedding.' He offered her the still warm brew, and she finally took it. Gently cradling it as she raised the cup to her nose and breathed in deeply, letting the tea's aroma fill her body with calm, a reminder that it wasn't the whole world that had been turned upside down that night. Just hers.

'You didn't think to tell me?' She gazed at him over the rim of the cup as she finally took a sip. Her eyes closed of their own accord and she made the most sinful of sounds as the light flowery taste bloomed over her tongue. He'd brewed it strongly, allowing the leaves to—

Her eyes flew open.

'This is from a bag.'

'Yes, and?' He smirked at her, highly bemused by the way she shifted in her seat.

'You said it was *mine*,' she pouted.

'It is,' he chuckled as he reached into the inside pocket of his jacket and pulled out a small tin. It held a few small bags of dark tea leaves. She gazed up at him confused. 'I asked your tea-guy to make a few bags for me. I figured with everything going on, I was going to have to make you a cup eventually.'

'And just when did you figure this?' she asked before taking another blissful sip.

'The night you were attacked and asked me to compile the dossier on Cormac.' The man sighed. 'He *wasn't* working for O'Malley, by the way, but O'Malley *was* trying to get him to. The guy refused every step of the way, even after the prick threatened to publish the pictures and reveal Cormac had been a stripper.'

'That was O'Malley?'

Marcus nodded.

'And then right after your honeymoon, he threatened him with the recording. Said he'd reveal that the two of you didn't know each other before the night of the attack. Again, Cormac told him you'd be able to get around it. But he was worried you'd find out about the deal. Do you know, he almost called off the wedding over the whole thing?'

'What!' Her eyes grew large, and she almost dropped the hot beverage in her lap at the revelation. 'When?'

'The day of. In fact, just a few minutes before he had to leave for the cathedral. He called me in, told me everything and said he couldn't marry you. That it wasn't fair to be hiding this from you.'

'And why didn't you tell me?' she shrieked, causing a nurse walking through the corridor to stop and stare. Warmth flushed Victoria's cheeks, and she shifted uncomfortably in the plastic seat. 'I mean,' she added, quieter. 'Why did you let him go through with it? Why didn't you tell me?'

Marcus paused, his lips pursing slightly as he considered her, weighing up his words carefully. It was something he'd done often when they'd been a couple, and it drove her absolutely mad.

'Why did you ask a man to marry you, whom you'd only met a few days before?'

She sucked in a breath, a whistling noise between her teeth as she realised his cleverness in avoiding her question. It wasn't something she was going to tell him—no matter how much friendlier they were—that remained between her and Cormac. And her sisters. And Mr Daven. And... Kirstie.

Something from the recording tickled her brain, something that O'Malley had said to Cormac...

My sources tell me that pretty soon you're going to receive an invitation to meet Her Ladyship, and I want you to do just that.

Someone in her circle had told Conner O'Malley she

wanted to meet Cormac *before* Cormac had been offered his deal. So even *if* Cormac was a leak, there was still someone else involved. And the only people to know about Cormac before she'd met with him to propose were Kirstie and Marcus. Marcus had never known about the plan, hadn't known *why* she had wanted the background check done on her husband. But Kirstie knew about her need to get married, and she'd known about her idea to *buy* a husband. And while Victoria hadn't shown her Cormac's dossier, she had *seen* it; Victoria had pulled it out to show her, and her secretary had watched where she'd shoved it afterwards. It wouldn't have taken much for her clever assistant to find it later, when the room was empty.

Kirstie was the only one who knew that she and Cormac would be at the house that night, alone, with enough time to tip someone off. The staff had been told to prepare the meal and make themselves scarce only that morning; it wasn't as if they'd been told that it would just be the happy couple in the house alone. For all they knew, James could have been there, or her sisters might have joined them... And *eleven* people, coordinated as they were, with exits covered, an idea of their escape route, how to get them to attempt that route...

'It's Kirstie,' she whispered. 'She's the leak.'

'What? You're sure?' Marcus asked, suddenly sitting up to attention.

'I'm positive,' she said.

Her private secretary, the woman she'd relied on for the last twelve years had been the one to betray her. She'd had no experience in such a role when she'd applied, but she'd had determination and drive and Victoria had liked that. Victoria had trusted her with every facet of her life; why had Kirstie done this?

'I'll get my men to bring her in immediately.'

Victoria nodded absently. She didn't even notice as he

stood up to make the call, trying to process the fact her secretary had nearly had her killed that evening. If it hadn't been for Cormac once again coming to her rescue...

'I love him, Marcus,' she finally confessed as he ended the call. He turned to her, his face softening as she lifted her eyes to his. 'What am I going to do if he doesn't make it?'

'He will,' Marcus told her firmly as he took his seat next to her again. He reached out and took her hand in his, giving it a squeeze of reassurance. 'He loves you too much not to.'

∽

VICTORIA, HER BODY TIRED AND WEARY AFTER SUCH A LONG night, sighed as she stepped off the lift into the softly lit lobby of the penthouse.

'Anything I can get you, my lady?' Merryweather asked as he stepped out to greet her. She offered him a small smile of thanks and shook her head.

'No, but thank you. Please, feel free to go back to bed,' she told him, knowing from the slightly haphazard way his tie was done that he'd thrown his uniform on the moment he'd been made aware of her arrival by the call of the lift.

'Very good, ma'am. Would you like a wakeup call?'

She rubbed her hand down her face as she considered her options. She could get up early and head back to Earlsbury General, sit and wait there until they finally gave in and let her visit Cormac in the ICU, or she could actually sleep in a bed, wake up refreshed and try and make a bit of sense out of everything.

She shook her head, and the butler gave her a small bow before retiring for the night. She watched him leave, staring at the door as it swung closed behind him, her mind completely blank as her body began to switch off, drained of all emotion, all thought, all desire to even move. Maybe she could just fall asleep here, and when morning came, she could just head back down again, dressed and ready to go...

'Victoria?'

Her name being softly called from the sitting room roused her from her mindless stare, reminding her that Alexi had been here all night. She rubbed the tiredness from her eyes before heading in to relieve her sister of babysitting duties.

'How are you?' Alexi asked as she walked in, her eyes filled with sympathy. Victoria made to answer but spied a sleeping James tucked up under a blanket on the other end of the sofa. Her heart broke all over again.

How much could this poor child go through? What would happen if Cormac didn't make it and he was left alone. Could she assume guardianship for James? Would the courts allow it?

She mentally shook herself at that thought; her grandfather was the King, he made the laws, he could damn well order the courts to make James her ward. And if he refused, well, she'd just have to cash in her biggest bargaining chip; revealing all those secrets that her cousin had poured out to her in his various drunken stupors and threatening to sell them off to the highest bidder.

And she'd bloody well do it too.

Although, now wasn't the time to think about that. She had to think the of best happening, not the worst.

'Why is he still up?' she asked instead of answering her sister.

Alexi glanced towards the sleeping child before turning back to her. 'He fell asleep while we were watching TV.' Alexi motioned towards the large screen television that was still on but set to mute. Her sister had her phone out, so she clearly hadn't been watching whatever she had on. 'You didn't answer my question.'

'How do I even begin to answer that?' she replied as she sank into the chair nearest to her baby sister. 'My husband is in critical condition; they don't know if he's going to pull through. Meanwhile, my secretary has been betraying me this whole time, feeding all my plans, every one of my movements to one of Daddy's competitors, and I have no idea why.' She threw herself back into the squishy chair and stared up at the ceiling.

'And all along, Cormac had been keeping all these secrets from me. Hiding the fact that Conner O'Malley had bribed him and has been trying to blackmail him all this time.'

She could feel Alexi's eyes, sad and sympathetic, staring at her from across the way. She wanted to tell her where to go, just as Marcus had to her earlier, but Alexi had been nothing but supportive from the moment she'd come up with her crazy *buying him* plan. She was the only one of her siblings who hadn't even questioned her choice of men, who hadn't told her that her idea was idiotic, who had actually praised her for going out and making it happen however she needed to. Just as their father would have.

Victoria reached out, her arm extended across the gap between chair and sofa, palm up, and Alexi took it without hesitation, squeezing her fingers, letting Victoria know she was there for her.

'So, he's stable?' Alexi asked softly after a moment and Victoria nodded. 'That's positive.' When Victoria said nothing, Alexi gripped her fingers tighter, making Victoria finally glance her way. 'It's a *good* sign, Tori, you need to hold onto that.'

'Don't call me that,' she muttered with a disapproving frown, but it was spiritless. 'They wouldn't let me see him.'

'They wouldn't? Did you try the whole *do you know who I am* shtick?'

Victoria bit her lip, ashamed to admit that she had, but

she'd been desperate to see him. To know with her own eyes that they were telling the truth, that he was still alive, even if he was wired up every way he could be.

'Wow, I would have loved to have seen that!' Alexi gave a half-hearted chuckle, before she sighed. 'Didn't work though?'

'Said that in medical matters, their say superseded my royal connections. Said even if the King marched in there, they'd deny him too.'

'Wow.' Silence fell between them, as each girl got lost in their own thoughts. 'I kinda want to see *that*,' Alexi finally admitted, breaking the quiet. Victoria huffed a small laugh.

'Me too.'

'Did you get any sleep while you were waiting?'

'Not really,' she admitted, resting her cheek on her shoulder. 'I tried for a little while, but the chairs were really uncomfortable. They need a relatives' room or something for people to wait in. Something with a couch or at least a reclining chair.'

'Maybe you should make a donation? Get one put in.'

'Yeah, maybe,' she agreed, but it wasn't really something to think about at that moment. Her eyes flickered over to where James lay, before lifting to the enormous Christmas tree that sat in the corner just behind him.

'It's Christmas Eve,' she muttered, remembering what day it was. 'It's Cormac's birthday.'

'Oh, Victoria.' Alexi got up and came over to her, crouching down before her and wiped away the tears she hadn't realised were falling. 'He will get through this,' she promised, but Victoria wished she wouldn't. She didn't want more lies, more broken promises and unfilled dreams.

'I love him, Alexi,' she whispered. 'I love him so much and it *hurts*.'

'I know, I know,' she cooed as she stroked her hair back.

'You'll get through this, we're all here for you, we'll all be at your side no matter what. I promise.'

Victoria nodded, trying to hold back the sobs that wanted to bubble up.

'Victoria?' James' sleepy voice called out and Victoria sucked in a deep breath, quickly wiping at the tears that marred her face.

'Hey, sweetie,' she said as she stood up and moved to sit beside him.

'Why are you here?' he asked as he sat up and rubbed the sleep out of his eyes. 'I thought I was meeting you and Dad in the morning?'

'Well, I came home because...' How the hell was she supposed to explain this to James?

'There's been an accident at the house, James,' Alexi said. She sat perched on the chair Victoria had just vacated.

'Yes,' Victoria said, jumping on that chain of thought. An accident was easier to explain than the whole complicated mess they were really in. 'I'm afraid that we've had to take Cormac to hospital.' That seemed to wake the child up completely. His eyes widened at her words and his little mouth dropped open slightly.

'Is he okay?' Victoria didn't think her heart could break any more than it already had that evening, but hearing the quiver in his voice, the fear and uncertainty laced within it, crushed whatever fragments were left.

'He's... The doctors are watching over him right now—'

'I want to see him.' James tried to get up off the couch. He was such a determined kid; he'd probably march himself downstairs and demand a car from the front desk to take him to see Cormac. Victoria quickly scooped his little frame up and settled him on her knee before he had the chance to scarper.

'I want to see Corrie!' he demanded as he tried to wiggle away from her.

'No, James,' she said firmly, gently grasping his chin in her hand so she could get him to face her. 'I'm so sorry, but you can't right now. He's terribly ill and the doctors, who are all *very* clever people, are doing absolutely *everything* they can to get him better as quickly as possible. But we must trust them and leave them to do their job, okay? And as soon as we're allowed to visit, we'll go straight there, alright?'

'You promise?' he asked. 'We'll go as soon as they say?'

'I promise.'

He stared at her, his hazel eyes searching hers, trying to spot any lies or half-truths she might be telling him. She wondered, not for the first time, how his brilliant little mind worked. She wasn't entirely sure if it was a blessing or a curse. Ask either of her genius sisters and they'd give two completely different answers.

'Is he going to die?' he whispered. His lower lip wobbled, and tears swam in his eyes.

'Oh, James.' Victoria brushed his hair back and pressed a kiss to his forehead. 'He's stable at the moment, but they need to keep him asleep for a long while so his body can recover. But as I said, they're doing everything they can to ensure that he wakes up as soon as possible.'

'I don't want him to die. I already lost my real mum and dad; Corrie can't die too!' he wailed before throwing himself into her embrace. He shook with sobs far too great for his little body. 'What's going to happen to me? Who's going to want me if Corrie isn't around?'

'Me,' she said without hesitation. 'I want you. Not just because of Cormac, but because I love you.'

James sniffled as he pulled back and looked up at Victoria. His face was red and swollen with his sobs, but his eyes held a mixture of hope and desperation.

'Really?'

'You asked a while ago if you could call me Mum. I know Cormac said he wanted to wait a while for that, but I just want you to know that I think of you as my own, my son, and when the time is right, you can call me Mum and I'll be very happy and very proud on that day.'

He gave her a watery smile before tucking himself back into her arms, holding onto her so tightly. She pressed another kiss to the crown of his head.

'I'll take care of you, no matter what. I promise, my little man.'

CHAPTER EIGHT

Victoria snapped closed her compact just as the car door opened. She stepped out and stared up at the towering, grey-stone building above her.

The Broken Hill.

Avalone's infamous, highest security prison. It was where the worst of the worst came... including those who had committed the crime of treason. It was a foreboding, ominous fortress built into the rocks of the Avon mountainside to camouflage it from the glistening city at its base. But the mere knowledge of its existence was a constant looming terror to Avon's residents, a reminder of the penalties awaiting them, should they turn their back on their country.

She'd never actually visited before despite being invited several times to attend treason hearings when she'd been involved—for example when Simon had attacked her—but she'd never accepted. Being there would mean they had managed to affect her, and Victoria never wanted them to think they had won in any way, shape, or form.

But today, today was different. Today she needed answers directly and not second hand as she usually got them. She took a deep breath before stepping forwards and climbing the steps to where Marcus stood waiting for her at the top.

'How are you?' he asked as she finally reached him. He leant down and wrapped her in a brief hug which she gratefully accepted.

'I'm okay.'

He eyed her sceptically at that comment. 'Really?'

'I'm *coping*, okay?' She fiddled with her bag as she spoke, avoiding his gaze. She was—just about—and only because she had James to look after. He kept her distracted as she tried to keep him from thinking of his brother, but it had been a difficult two weeks with school being closed for the Christmas holidays.

Every day, after she'd called the hospital and told her young charge there was no change, he'd start crying again, begging her to promise him once more that he wouldn't be put in a boarding home, that she wouldn't leave him like everyone else.

He'd started wetting the bed again too, Merryweather had reported, so Victoria began falling asleep with him on the couch in the living room. It seemed being snuggled up against her was reassuring to his sleeping form, and for the last few nights, he'd thankfully not had an accident.

'How's Cormac doing?'

She heaved a sigh. Marcus was like a starving dog with a bone, and while she knew such tenacity was a much-needed trait for his job, it wasn't appreciated by her. He never knew where to draw the line. It had caused a fair number of arguments between them when they'd been together.

'The same. No change, which is apparently a positive thing. They're moving him from the ward to a private room tomorrow and I'll finally be allowed to visit him.'

Victoria was both relieved and terrified at the news she'd received on her way over. She, of course, wanted Cormac to live, to wake up, and get better, but the closer that became a reality meant there was a greater urgency for her to make a decision about what she was going to do about their marriage. Did she muddle through holding it over him until they had a child and then end it? Should she give everything up and just end it immediately—could she live with a liar? Or should she forgive him and move on with their lives, accept that he loved her and admit her own feelings too? She had no idea and she really didn't want to face such choices.

Not today.

Not any time soon.

'That's good,' Marcus said with a bob of his head.

'Yes, well, it's about time. Shall we?' she asked, gesturing towards the large black doors they stood before, but the man made no effort to move.

'How was Christmas?'

'Seriously, Marcus, are we having afternoon tea or going to visit a prisoner?'

She really didn't want to admit that Christmas day had been a sad affair, the worst she'd ever had, and that included the first one after her mother had died.

James had flat out refused to open his presents, saying he wanted Corrie there to see him. She'd spent the day trying to periodically encourage him to open at least one, hoping to see a little smile on his face. Then, after almost burning down the kitchen when she'd tried to cook the two of them breakfast, she'd had to call Merryweather back into action. She'd apologised profusely to the butler, knowing he was supposed to be off work for the holiday period due to the fact they weren't supposed to be residing in the super-suite any longer.

And in between trying to get James to open his presents, ensuring he didn't have a chance to cry, and keeping him distracted as best she could from lingering on thoughts of his brother, she'd been on the phone with the house staff, explaining what had happened and asking them to begin work on putting it back to rights as soon as the investigation had finished. She didn't want any evidence left of what had transpired there that night, didn't want to see a single drop of blood, shard of glass, or trampled flower. She didn't care if they had to replace the flooring, repaint the walls or dig up bushes; it had to be exactly as it was. She didn't want any sort of reminder there to trigger Cormac, or even herself, when they finally moved back home.

By the end of the day, she was utterly exhausted. She'd wanted nothing more than to climb in the tub with a large gin and tonic and think of nothing. But James had been clingy that night and it wasn't until the following day she'd managed to grab just the quickest of showers, and that was only because Alexi had popped over and distracted her young charge long enough for her to feel semi-human again.

On New Year's Eve, her sisters had come over and she'd got so blind drunk she'd fallen into the pool fully clothed and woken up the next morning sniffling after sleeping on a sun lounger in just her underwear. The three had agreed to stay over and help with James the following morning, giving her a chance to have a break and bury her head in the sand for a few hours.

'Look, I'm just surprised you're actually here,' the Head of the Guard admitted as he led them towards the giant doors. 'You've never attended a hearing before, and I *know* you've certainly never even entertained the idea of meeting with a prisoner. So, I just want to make sure that your head is in the right place.'

'None have been this close to home,' she confessed as a tiny door within the larger one opened. Marcus had to duck his head to get through the narrow opening. 'And I feel this one… This isn't one I can just brush off. This hurts in more ways than one.'

Marcus glanced towards her, his face sympathetic before he turned to the men waiting inside and handed over the file he was holding.

'Lady Blake is here to see prisoner 56713-KCB279.'

'Not a Lady for much longer,' she reminded him. At the end of February, her time as a working royal would be over and she'd soon be able to settle down into a life that focused on her family… If she still had one.

He gave her a glance from the corner of his eye that told her to *shut up*. She frowned back at him; she was glad they were becoming friends, but she wasn't totally on board with this new attitude he had towards her.

'Your grandfather has eyes and ears all over this place,' he muttered as he stepped back to her side while the prison officers took the paperwork away to check through it. 'Until you're in the visitors' room, and until I give you the all-clear, I suggest you say nothing else.'

Victoria narrowed her eyes at the Guardsman but remained quiet as per his *suggestion*.

The prison officers returned and led them through a series of corridors, finally stopping at an unassuming door.

'You'll be alone, as per your request, my lady,' the officer said.

'Thank you,' she replied as he opened the door for her.

'And I'll be the only one in the observation room—behind the glass,' Marcus added. 'And I'll have the microphones switched off as you asked.' She gave Marcus a nod before stepping into the room.

It was a small grey room that offered no comfort. The large circular table seemed to fill the space and only two chairs remained around it. She glanced towards the mirror that almost filled the wall, wondering if Marcus was behind it already.

Suddenly, the mirror became transparent as Marcus flicked the light on inside the observation room.

'I want you to sit in the chair nearest the door, but wait here, by the window until they arrive. When she's seated and the guard has left, *then* take the seat, okay?'

'Okay,' she said, her stomach suddenly churning with nerves. She glanced around for something to comment on, but the room held little for way of conversation.

'Why's the table round? In the films they're always rectangular.'

'So, there's no sharp edges or corners that could be used to seriously hurt someone if a prisoner decided to attack.'

That made sense, she reasoned. She was about to ask why the shows got that wrong when the door opened and a Broken Hill officer walked in, his prisoner shuffling along behind him in a jangle of handcuffs and shackle chains.

Kirstie, her former private secretary, had always been perfectly presented. Smart skirt suits and high heels, her make up in a natural style—never overly done—and her hair always tied up in a French plait or neat little bun. Now, she was dressed in an unflattering vivid-pink prison uniform, her hair hanging limply around her bare face. She looked pale, almost sickly, purple rings under her eyes were the only colour that adorned her face, and she hunched in on herself. She was a shadow of her former self and part of Victoria's heart went out to the woman before she reminded herself *why* Kirstie was in such a situation.

She watched the guards seat her former secretary, connecting her handcuffs to the table.

'Does she really need them?' Victoria asked, noticing there were red marks around her slim wrists.

'She's in for high treason, ma'am, it's standard protocol,' the first officer told her.

'She sold information, she didn't try and scale the palace to murder the King. Take them off.'

The two officers looked at each other, neither one wanting to disobey her, but also not wanting to go against protocol.

'It's okay,' Marcus said from the other side of the glass. 'I'll accept the responsibility.' The officers shrugged before complying, and Victoria watched as the chains and cuffs were removed.

'And her feet.' That got her another glance. She refrained from rolling her eyes, but her tone of voice made it clear she wanted to. 'It's not as if she's going to be able to run away.'

The officers once more obliged, taking the shackles off, before they left, the clanking of the metal leaving with them.

'Thank you,' Kirstie said quietly after the door closed behind them. Victoria turned to Marcus, nodding at him, and she watched him lean over and press a button she assumed controlled the microphone before he switched the light off, turning the glass back into a mirror. She knew he was still standing behind it, but she hoped without him visible, Kirstie might be more inclined to speak up.

With a measured step, Victoria walked to the seat Marcus had told her to take, her eyes focused on the woman opposite who refused to raise her head and meet Victoria's gaze. Instead, Kirstie stared down at the table, her fingers gently rubbing at her wrists where the cuffs had chaffed her skin raw.

'You know I don't normally do this,' Victoria began. 'I mean, you know I don't even attend the trials, never mind sit opposite a traitor'—Kirstie visibly flinched at the word which Victoria found interesting—'and ask them *why*. But here I am.'

Kirstie bobbed her head, but still didn't look Victoria's way.

Victoria waited a few moments, her fingers drumming on the table in impatience, before she sighed and gave in. They were limited on time and she wanted to get her answers.

'Why, Kirstie? Why did you sell me out?' No answer. 'Was it something I said? Something I did? Did I hurt you in some way? Mistreat you?'

The woman slowly shook her head before Victoria heard the unmistakeable sound of a sniffle. Was she crying because she felt guilty or because she'd been caught? Or perhaps it was all an act, just as she'd been acting like a loyal friend this whole time.

'When did you start working for O'Malley?'

Kirstie raised her head a little. She stared at Victoria through her limp, dark hair, her deep, brown eyes red-ringed, made her look even paler than earlier.

'Is this being recorded?' she asked, her voice thick with emotion.

Victoria shook her head. 'Whatever is said in here, stays in here.'

'What about *him*?' Kirstie nodded towards the mirror. 'Is he listening in?'

Again, Victoria shook her head. 'As I said, what's said in here, stays in *here*.' She jabbed the table with her finger to emphasis her point. 'I want answers, Kirstie. I trusted you with so much, I need to know everything.'

Kirstie swallowed, still hesitant to reveal her secrets.

'Kirstie, why did you set us up? What did we do that was so bad you were willing to have a hand in *murder*? Why did—'

'What?' Victoria suddenly had the other woman's full attention. Her face was filled with genuine confusion at her words. 'Murder? No, that wasn't part of the plan.'

Victoria leaned forward, her gaze unwavering as she told Kirstie what had happened that fateful night.

'One of them came at me,' she revealed. 'He had a knife. He was going to stab me with it, but Cormac got in the way.'

'No!' Kirstie gasped. 'No! They said that there wouldn't be any harm to either of you.'

'Well, they lied.'

'No,' Kirstie shook her head. 'That wasn't... It wasn't supposed to be that way.'

'Then what was supposed to happen?'

'They were supposed to scare you, get you in a position where you *had* to listen to what they had to say. They wanted your marriage destroyed, wanted to watch the fall out knowing they'd done that, to see the nation's sweethearts get knocked off their perch.'

Victoria's frown deepened. 'But *why?*'

'Because... Because Cormac wouldn't play their game,' Kirstie finally admitted, throwing up her hands. 'If he'd have just told O'Malley right from the start what you'd offered— or at least something *more* than a lunch date—none of this would have happened. He'd have been done; *I'd* have been done...' The woman buried her face in her hands. 'Why didn't he just tell him?'

Cormac had been telling the truth. Victoria blinked as she processed that bit of information. He might have accepted the deal, but he hadn't followed through on it. However, that still didn't explain how that tied into the woman sitting opposite her.

'Why would Cormac revealing to O'Malley my proposal get *you* out of whatever you got yourself into... No,' Victoria paused. 'Start at the beginning; how and *why* did you even get involved with that son of a bitch?'

Kirstie sighed and lifted her gaze to the ceiling. She was

always very careful in her words, and Victoria could see she was fighting a war within herself.

'I have a brother, Geoffrey,' she finally began, surprising Victoria. She didn't recall that on the security information she'd had on her assistant, and Kirstie had never mentioned him before now. 'Well, he's actually a distant cousin, but my parents raised him so he's more of a sibling. It was always hard on him, knowing that his mum didn't want him, and I guess that's what got him into so much trouble. Mum and Dad kept bailing him out, paying off whatever debts he racked up so the loan sharks or the bookies wouldn't hurt him.'

Kirstie sighed deeply and lowered her gaze back down to the table. She ran her fingers over a few scratches in the wood as she gathered herself together for whatever was to come next, but Victoria just wanted to shake her. To scream *tell me!* so this could all be over and done with and she could walk out of here and never think of her former assistant again.

However, right now, Victoria needed to know why, to understand how Conner O'Malley was able to get to someone like Kirstie. Cormac she could understand; he was broke, he had a little brother to care for, he was desperate, but Kirstie... Kirstie had everything, a well-paying, highly connected job that came with so many benefits—travelling the world, entry to exclusive parties, being in the know about almost *everything*—how did O'Malley get to someone like that?

'When Dad passed away, it got really bad,' Kirstie all but whispered. 'Geoff moved back in with Mum and basically...' Her voice cracked and she ran her hands over her face as if she could rub away whatever bad memories the story held.

'He was supposedly back on the wagon; he'd been sober for months, hadn't gambled in over a year, it was all going well for him. I even managed to get him a job, just groundskeeping for the local council but it was outdoors, which was what he liked, and it kept him busy. *Busy hands make it harder for the devil to tempt you,* my mother used to say.

'I thought it was all going well and then when Mum died... Well, I got a wakeup call. He'd somehow managed to get her to sign the house over to him, which was now mortgaged to the hilt, her savings were gone, her pension cashed in... I found out he hadn't been going to work, that he'd lost the jobs months before and that he had so much debt... He came to me after Mum's funeral, frightened for his life and—' She hiccupped on a sob and Victoria had to stop herself reaching out to the woman she had once considered a kind of friend. She had no idea Kirstie's mother hadn't had an estate. The woman had died a few months before her own father, and she'd retreated into mourning. Just as she'd returned, Victoria's own father had passed away and the woman just threw herself into her job.

'I told him tough. That he'd stolen everything from me!' Kirstie's fingers curled into fists, and Victoria knew Kirstie was trying to keep her temper under control. 'My parents had wasted so much time, effort, and money on him, trying to get him back on the right path and all he'd done was wasted his life, thrown away their efforts and goodwill. Well, he wasn't having mine!'

She slammed her fist down on the table, making Victoria flinch.

The light behind the glass flickered on, and the two women turned to see Marcus frowning back at them. Kirstie glared at the Head of the Guard, and Victoria was surprised at the palpable anger she saw from the woman; she'd thought the two had always got on very well in the past. But now wasn't the time to question that. She wanted to get to the bottom of the O'Malley thing.

Victoria waved Marcus away, and thankfully he switched the light off again, leaving the two women to their semi-private state.

'I'm sorry to hear those things about... Geoff? But how does that link you to Conner O'Malley?'

Kirstie slowly refocused her attention on Victoria and met her gaze for the first time since she'd entered the room.

'I didn't hear from Geoff for a few weeks, then one day I got a finger delivered to me. Geoff's little finger.'

Victoria gasped. 'What?'

'It had a note, pay up or the rest would be delivered over the next several days.' Kirstie glanced away again. 'I didn't have enough to give them. You'—she took a deep breath—'weren't paying me anymore, and I'd already eaten into a good chunk of my savings because of it.'

Victoria sat back in her chair and assessed the woman before her. Her brown eyes shimmered with tears, and her lower lip was caught between her teeth to stop it from wobbling. Victoria wondered why she'd thought she had to go through all that alone.

'Why didn't you tell me? Or at least go to the Guard?'

'You didn't have the money,' she said quietly. 'And the Guard... they'd have made me stand down, and I couldn't leave you when you needed me so much.'

'Stand down? Why? Who told you—' Victoria cut herself off as she glared at the mirror.

'I called Marcus, and I asked him *hypothetically* what to do if I knew a staff member was in my position. All he did was demand to know who it was because they needed cutting out right away. Cutting out,' she scoffed at the word. 'As if it was a bad piece of a potato. I had to tell him it was merely for us to update our security risk assessments. He told me to contact the admin desk in that case and stop wasting his time.'

Victoria gripped the table as she took a deep breath and side-eyed the mirror again. No wonder Kirstie had such ire towards the man behind the glass. She and Marcus were certainly going to have to have a long discussion later regarding this particular matter. Staff had to feel safe coming to them when problems like this arose. How many others might be compromised because they felt they were going to be *cut out?*

'Okay, so you didn't have the money, and no one was willing to support you. You were trapped. So how did that translate to... *this?*'

'I called the number and told them I only had some of the money to cover the debt at that moment and that I could get the rest, but it would take a little while. They didn't want to hear it, but then someone else came on the phone—'

'O'Malley?'

Kirstie nodded, her gaze once more meeting hers. 'He said I could pay in another way and we arranged a meeting. When we met, he told me he wanted information on you, specific information relating to the will and your father's company. I told him I wasn't privy to that and he gave me Geoff's other little finger.'

'Bloody hell!' Victoria was truly horrified. The man had *already* cut her cousin's finger off before their meeting *just in case* she couldn't give him what he wanted. What sort of monster were they dealing with?

'I told him that I'd get it, that I'd find out *something.*'

'But you already knew everything,' Victoria said, puzzled as to why she hadn't just spilt everything to the man there and then.

'I didn't want to betray you; I didn't want to get involved with the likes of him. I thought that if I could buy Geoff a little time, I could figure something out. Perhaps, if I got you married off quickly, you could lend me the money for the rest of the debt.'

'And all the interest O'Malley would add to it.' Another solemn nod.

'I got a message the next day telling me that I better have something soon or there'd be another piece delivered... This time, to the office. So, I said that you were suddenly extremely interested in dating, and that you were asking me to set you up on several dates with different men... Then came Simon.'

'But Alexi introduced me to Simon.'

'Yes, but who do you think nudged her in that direction?'

'Simon?' Kirstie nodded.

'From what I understand, Simon was beholden to O'Malley for the turn in his fortunes. He drugged you at his request. You were supposed to pass out in a car, and they were going to take compromising pictures of you and him together.'

Victoria closed her eyes and breathed in deeply through her nose, holding it for a moment and counting to five before she released it again.

'That utter bastard,' she muttered.

'That's *why* there was a photographer nearby. When you didn't drink the whole glass and were able to run, it threw their plans off kilter. When Cormac interrupted Simon, the bastard messaged the photographer, told him it was off, but then the 'tog decided he could at least make a few crowns from getting you coming out of a strip club... and it didn't take much to put two and two together that the next stop would be hospital.

'When you—' Kirstie stopped and looked towards the mirror again. 'Are you sure he can't hear us?' Victoria's brows raised at that. Even now, she was clearly concerned with Marcus hearing something she didn't want him to know.

'Positive. If he dared, I'd ruin him.' They might be forming a friendship, but it wasn't as if they were BFFs or whatever the latest phrase was that Alexi threw around. Kirstie nodded.

'When you came to me with the idea of *buying a husband*'—she whispered the latter part—'I tried to talk you out of it because I didn't want to report that to O'Malley and give him a way to get to you. But I saw Cormac's name on the file, and I did a little digging, found out he was employed at that strip club where you were saved. I messaged O'Malley and said that I might be able to point him in the direction of finding out more about your father's will, and if I could, would that be enough. He said yes, but if I couldn't, I'd owe him twice the price.'

'You told him about Cormac rescuing me and that I wanted to meet with him.'

'I told him you had a *proposal* to make, and he got the gist. I thought...' Kirstie sighed. 'I thought Cormac would tell him and I'd be free. I wouldn't have been the one to betray you, but someone you just met, someone you shouldn't have trusted with such information... But he backed out. He told O'Malley you just took him to dinner, and he went ballistic...'

The tears Kirstie had been holding back began to fall freely. She tried to speak, but the words wouldn't come, and Victoria decided to screw the rules and leaned across the table, taking Kirstie's hands in her own. The other woman grasped them back, holding onto her as if her life depended on it.

'They found Geoff two days later,' she managed to get out. 'I had to go and identify him. That was the funeral I had to arrange.'

'Oh, Kirstie, *why* didn't you come to me by that point? I had access to my inheritance, I could have got you out.'

'How?' Kirstie stared at her with wide, pleading eyes. 'How could I come and tell you that I'd betrayed you? That I'd broken your trust and ruined our friendship? You wouldn't have helped; you'd have done exactly what Marcus had said and cut me out. You *hate* O'Malley; you hate anyone that works with him or *for* him.'

'You could have explained to me, like you are now—'

'And how much did you war with yourself to come here today? You *never* face those who have tried to hurt you; you never want them to see they affected you. You even said it when I came in. You wouldn't have listened by that point.'

A wave of guilt washed over Victoria as she recognised Kirstie spoke the truth. It had taken almost the entire two weeks to decide she would come today.

'You're right,' she said. 'But I'm here now.'

'I'm not finished, Victoria. Just because they killed Geoff didn't mean I was let off the hook. Cormac hadn't paid up, so I carried a bigger debt because I'd got him involved, even though he had his own price to pay for *not* betraying you. I don't…' She sighed. 'I don't think I ever would have paid the debt back, truth be told. Once he has his claws in you that's it, you're his for life, whether you like it or not.

'I gave him Cormac's number, that's how he messaged him.'

'He was messaging Cormac?'

'From what I understand. But it wasn't working; he still wouldn't play ball.'

A light flickered on in Victoria's mind. 'Did you release the photos?'

'No.' Kirstie shook her head. 'That was all O'Malley. He owns the club through a number of interlinking businesses. Keeps the unsavoury ones from contaminating his more prestigious brands.'

'But you told him about Cormac and me being in the house, alone, that night.'

Kirstie pulled her hands away from Victoria's and sat back in her seat. She nodded as she stared at the floor.

'As I said, he told me he just wanted to split you two up. That neither of you would get hurt, and that after this I was done, I was free of him. No more debt, no more favours, no more betrayals. I'd been living with that yoke on my shoulders for almost nine months, the idea of it being gone, of finally being free... I took the offer.

'I gave him the date you would both be there, without anyone knowing and without James—that was one condition I said couldn't be broken. James wasn't to be there and if he was, he had to call it off. If I found out that James had been there and it had gone ahead, I told him I'd tell the Guard everything.'

'So why don't you want Marcus hearing this?'

'Because...' she glanced at the mirror again. 'I found out just a few weeks before my mum died that I have a niece. A beautiful little girl that Geoff accidentally gave to some poor woman. O'Malley said that if I reveal *anything* to the Guard, the police, *anyone*, then she'd pay the price.'

Victoria's hand flew up to her mouth as she gasped. What monster would threaten a *child*?

'Kirstie, we have *got* to get him,' Victoria pleaded. 'If not for you, but for your niece, for the other people out there that are under his thumb that shouldn't be. How many more Geoffs have there been? How many more families pulled into his schemes because of *debts* that are owed?

'We can do it, Kirstie, and I promise, you will be protected the whole way.'

'I don't care about me, just as long as Penny is safe...'

'But she won't be while *he's* out there,' Victoria tried to reason. 'There'll be ways he'll get to you in here. What if he goes to Penny's mum and pulls her into all this?'

Kirstie's head snapped up at that.

'Do it for Penny,' she urged.

Kirstie bit her lip as she considered Victoria's request. Her eyes drifted over towards the mirror one last time.

'For Penny,' she agreed.

∼

Victoria sat in the Royal Box, watching the proceedings with interest. She'd never actually been in a court before, but she was sure the one here at the Broken Hill wasn't the same as elsewhere in the country. There were no trials by jury here; instead, five judges—the Royal Justices—sat and presided over the case and decided the punishment based on the evidence. Many countries didn't understand, calling it draconian and barbaric, that it was against human rights, blah, blah, blah, but it had worked this way for over two centuries and was ingrained into their heritage.

The Royal Justices were the best judges in all Avalone and were highly respected throughout the nation. They had spent hours in courtrooms as barristers and had to have presided over hundreds of cases as a regular judge in the lower courts and the Crown Courts before you were even eligible to be considered for the prestigious role. There were twelve Royal Justices at any one time, and once appointed, it was a job for life; only retirement or death allowed a vacancy to open. Thankfully, they weren't called upon often and most of their job was spent researching laws and advising King Richard on legal issues across the land and those developing internationally that may affect Avalone in some way.

She'd met a few of the Justices when attending royal events and had found them insightful and generally courteous. But seeing them now, seated behind the bench in all their court finery, they seemed imposing and intimidating, and she was glad she wasn't the one in the dock.

She hadn't looked at Kirstie throughout the whole hearing, not even when she had pleaded guilty with a quiver in her voice.

'Before we pass sentence, Lady Snape, would you like to speak?'

Victoria slowly rose from her seat, her palms already sweating as all eyes turned to her. Even though she had nothing to feel guilty over, the penetrating stares of the judges high above her made her feel as if she were somehow in the wrong, and she knew that her words were being listened to very carefully. She swallowed; what she said here and now could make or break their plan.

'It's Blake, but yes, Your Honours.'

'Do you wish to bestow your good grace on the defendant, Lady Blake?' a second judge asked.

Victoria licked her lips and nodded.

'Yes, Your Honours. As you are aware, I have had the misfortune of receiving many invites to attend this court and bestow my grace on several guilty parties, and I have always refused. Therefore, I hope that my presence today already speaks volumes as to the will of my grace. However, if it does not, I would like to say that Miss Berk has been my private secretary and my... friend for almost fifteen years. In that time, she was a loyal and trustworthy person and it is unfortunate and a deep shame that she let me down, and most of all let herself down, in the last days of her career. This is something she will have to live with for the rest of her life. Her career is over, her reputation is ruined, and her future, which was once bright, is now all but extinguished.

'I am here today to request that you judge her fairly, but not overly harsh. She has been a loyal servant to the Crown up until recently, ensuring that my duties were performed, that my security was handled, and even in assisting me with personal matters. Throughout all this, save for this one, albeit, costly error, she has kept my privacy and confidence, and I never once had cause to doubt her.' Victoria took a deep breath as she met the eyes of each judge, none of whom gave anything away, their faces as stoic as they had been throughout the hearing.

'We all make mistakes in life,' she continued. 'Unfortunately, hers are greater than others. I bestow my good grace on her, as is my right as the injured party, and by royal prerogative would ask for the minimum term you can give her within the law, to be halved, Your Honours, for her previous good work, my personal feelings, and my royal birth right.'

'Duly noted, Lady Blake,' the first judge said. 'We acknowledge your graces and accept your royal prerogative. However, you are only half of the injured party, I understand that your husband is still in critical condition in Earlsbury General.'

'He is stable, Your Honour; he has been downgraded from critical today.' That nervous-guilty feeling tugged at her once again.

'That is good to hear.' The judge looked down the line of his peers who all nodded to him. 'Very well, my lady, your good grace and royal rights will be considered as part of our sentencing. Thank you.'

She nodded and quickly took her seat again, thankful that her shaking knees had kept her standing throughout. She glanced to Marcus who sat in the gallery; he nodded at her and she huffed a sigh of relief that she'd done okay.

'Sentencing will be held tomorrow at 3pm,' a third judge said, before banging her gavel. 'Court adjourned.'

The five judges stood up and left the room one after the

other, before anyone else began to gather their things. Victoria caught sight of Kirstie being led from the dock, her head bowed and her shoulders once more hunched up as she withdrew in on herself. She had to be punished, there was no doubt about it, and her career was over and done with. When she was finally released, she would have to start all over again and Victoria knew it would be difficult for her to get any sort of well-meaning work with a criminal record, let alone one citing the crime of treason.

A heavy weight settled in Victoria's heart at the thought. What would she have done in such a situation?

'Well done,' Marcus said as he joined her. 'You did very well. I think they'll do as you asked.'

'And how long do you think she'll get?'

'Hard to say, maybe ten years.'

'*Ten!*'

'They may reduce it again if Cormac speaks for her when he recovers.'

'*If,*' she muttered.

'Don't be like that,' he chided.

She narrowed her eyes at him, but knew he was right. She had to be more optimistic in her thoughts, but right now she just wanted to go home and rest, and not have to think about anything else for the next few hours.

'Is everything set to proceed?' she asked as they watched the barristers and solicitors begin to leave the room. 'Will she be protected in here?'

'I've spoken to the warden; she'll be put into protective custody. We'll say it's for her own safety.'

'Good. I need you to get that bastard,' she told him. 'No excuses. Make sure that when you get him, you take him alive. I want to see *him* standing in that dock.'

'I'm sure with Kirstie's help, we'll get him.'

She rubbed her forehead as she tried to make sense of

everything. She hadn't realised how hard Kirstie's tale would hit her, how much she'd feel for her former secretary or how much she wanted to help the woman who had betrayed her.

But at least now, she had some understanding of how Cormac had got caught up in the web that O'Malley had spun.

'I need to get back to James.' She grabbed her bag as she stood up. She began to step out of the box but stopped, turning back to the Head of the Guard as she remembered something. 'And we'll be having words over the whole part *you* played in throwing her into O'Malley's waiting arms soon. Understand?'

'Yes, my lady,' he said as he ducked his head in shame. She nodded once, before turning to leave the court, knowing that although it was unfair to hold it against him, having not been aware of the whole picture, his transgression might not be so easy to forgive. How many others had tried to find help from the people who were supposed to be protecting them and found nothing but threats? How many others were being pushed into situations like Kirstie had found herself in? It didn't have to be as extreme as the one she'd faced; anything that caused them to worry or stress was enough, and Victoria wanted to ensure that everyone who needed help got it.

'Victoria?' She sighed as she stopped at the call of her name. She turned to him, holding out her hand in a *what* gesture. He looked unsure, and that gave Victoria pause.

'We got the name of the man who had the knife, the one who attacked you.'

'The one who stabbed Cormac,' she corrected.

'Yes,'

'Good, now go find him.'

'Don't you want to know who it was?'

She opened her mouth, about to retort that it didn't matter; as long as he got his comeuppance, that was all she cared about, but something in the way he refused to meet her gaze made her hesitate.

Did she need to know? Was it another leak?

'Go on.'

'Ben Fuller.'

Victoria's knees went weak and she grabbed onto the little door to the box to steady herself.

Ben, her stalker, the man who had made her life hell a few years ago after she and Marcus had called it quits. He had been deemed mentally unfit for trial and instead had been remanded into custody of a psychiatric ward.

'No, it can't be. He's in a psych ward down in Fanechester!' she protested.

'He was. He was released a few months ago.'

'What? Why didn't I know? Did you keep this from me in another attempt to "protect" me?'

'No, we weren't alerted. Don't worry,' he said before she could start another tirade. 'I've spoken to the authorities there and taken them to task already.'

'*That's* not what I'm worried about!' she told him, staring at him with wide eyes, her arms flung open. 'You have to get him! I can't go through that again. I can't be watching my back every time I leave the house, or wondering if I'm being watched when in my own garden, and I have James and Cormac to think about and—'

'Victoria.' He stood up and grasped her shoulders gently, making her stop her panicked outburst. 'We already have him and *this time,* he won't be getting out again. I'll make sure of it.'

'Thank you,' she whispered, nodding her head as if to reassure herself. 'Thank you.'

A DOCTOR HAD GREETED THEM OUTSIDE CORMAC'S ROOM AND explained the situation to her—where the knife had penetrated, how something had caused an infection, why he was still unconscious—but she hadn't really been listening, distracted by the Guards posted on either side of the doors. Where they there as general royal protection or because there was still a threat to Cormac's life? That last question set her on edge all over again.

Victoria had no idea what she was expecting when she'd walked into the hospital room that afternoon, James huddled against her leg, but seeing her husband pale against the hospital sheets, wires and tubes sticking out of what looked like everywhere, was certainly not it.

'Dad?' James whispered, his little voice broken, as he spied his brother for the first time. When there wasn't even a flicker of reaction from Cormac the young boy burst into tears.

'Oh, James!' Victoria scooped him up in her arms and held him close, cradling his head as he buried his face into her neck and sobbed freely.

'He's never going to get better,' his terrified voice whispered between heaving breaths. 'He's going to sleep forever and ever.'

'No, no, he will,' she said, her voice soft and soothing as she rubbed her hand up and down his back. 'He's already improved, remember? He's been moved from where the sickest people are into his own room! It's just going to take some time.' But the boy was shaking his head, the feeling of snot smearing against her skin, made her cringe, but it was a small price to pay for the trust he put in her.

'He's never going to get better, he's never—and it's my fault!'

Well, that certainly surprised her.

She leaned back, gently pulling James away from her so that she could see his face. 'What's that supposed to mean?'

'I- I—' He began to wiggle, kicking and squirming to be put down. 'Let me go,' he begged pushing at her arms and she quickly complied.

'Corrie,' he called as he hurried to his brother's side, but stayed a step back from the bed, his young, scared eyes, brightened with tears, following from the cannula in Cormac's hand up his arm to his brother's sleeping face. 'I promise not to call you dad any more if you wake up.'

Victoria gasped, a deep inhale of breath as her already battered and bruised heart, broke just that little bit more.

'I don't need a dad, I can have a Corrie,' he carried on. 'I promise. I promise I'll never ask again, I'll never ask you to be my dad ever, ever again—'

'James.' Victoria gently took his hand as she crouched down to his side. 'That's not why he's not waking up,' she told him softly. 'He had an infection, and his body is resting after fighting it off. It's not your fault, Cormac loves you very, very much, so much so he wants to be your dad. He'd be very upset to hear what you just said.'

His hazel eyes widened at her words, and his head snapped around to look back at his brother. 'I'm sorry!' he wailed and Victoria wanted to swear. Instead, she pulled her to him again, picked him up and made to leave.

She paused as one of the Guardsmen opened the door, glancing back over her shoulder to where her husband slept on, hopefully oblivious to what had just occurred. She took him in for a second, her eyes scanning his mused hair, the stubble on his cheeks, his broad shoulders, and strong arms that had held her so tightly on so many nights after they'd made passionate love…

She swallowed, wondering if they'd ever have those moments again. That even if they could move past what he'd done, even if she could in some way forgive him, could they be how they were once again?

And if they couldn't… How would the little boy in her arms take it?

∽

She hadn't brought James back. She wasn't sure if that was the right thing to do or not, but after their last visit, she hadn't wanted to risk it. The boy had been through enough in such a short space of time, he needed some normality, so she'd took him to school, seeing him off with a wave, before having Toby bring her by Earlsbury General.

But now that she was stood here, her back against the door, watching the shallow rise and fall of her husband's chest, she wasn't sure if it had been the right thing to do. What exactly could she do here other than sit in silence and stare at her sleeping beauty?

Victoria turned, her vision swimming with tears, and yanked open the door. She ignored the concerned calls from the Guards as she all but ran from the room, never once glancing back.

∽

Tick. Tick. Tick. Tick.

Victoria's eye twitched in time with the second hand of the clock. Her fingers curled under the hem of her skirt as she continued to count down the seconds until she could get up and leave.

Tick. Tick. Tick. Tick.

Her eyes flickered towards Cormac before moving away again, refocusing on the linen of his bed. She traced the pattern on the pale blue blanket for the fiftieth time that morning before once more lifting her gaze to check the time.

Eight minutes and fifteen seconds. A new record.

She slipped her fingers under the hand of her bag and made to stand when the door to Cormac's room swung open.

'Ah, Lady Snape—'

'It's Blake,' Victoria corrected automatically.

'Apologies, Lady Blake.' The young woman held up her hands. 'I'm so glad that I caught you today, I keep seeming to miss you.'

Victoria frowned but heat filled her cheeks that her short visits had been noted. 'And you are?' She offered no apology, as a member of the Royal Family, she was never to apologize.

'Doctor Woods, I've been taking care of your husband.' The woman gave her a beaming smile and Victoria wasn't sure if she was expecting a thank you or a pat on the head. She recalled how the sycophant doctors used to linger around her mother, plying her with platitudes of how well she was doing simply to get some form of acknowledgement of their worth from her.

And when her mother had died, Victoria had learnt well from their lies, that doctors could not be trusted.

Victoria gave Cormac the quickest of glances—her stomach still churned with a wash of conflicting emotions—and then levelled her stare back at this so called doctor.

'He looks worse every day; I'd suggest you do a better job.'

'We're keeping him under sedation to beat the infection and to help his body recuperate,' Doctor Woods advised, her jovial tone turning slightly more professional. 'Lady Blake, your husband has been through the works; we almost lost him twice.'

Victoria's shoulder's straightened at such a revelation, her eyes widen slightly and her breathing became so shallow and slow she almost forgot to breathe. 'I'm sorry, what?'

'Lady Blake, please sit down.' The physical motioned to the chair she'd been sat on just a few moments ago, while the doctor took the one next to her. 'When he arrived, he was on the brink of death from losing so much blood. The knife punctured through his abdominal muscles, and his lower intestine; which, as you can imagine, is not a good thing. Not only did his body have to try and recover from the puncture wounds, it's also had to fight off several infections. We thought he was coming through it last night, but unfortunately he took another turn; sepsis, and sepsis shock is not something to gloss over or brush off. He's a very lucky man.'

Victoria took a deep breath as it began to really hit home the severity of Cormac's plight. She'd known he'd been close to death on the night. She'd witnessed him passing out, scrubbed his blood from her skin afterwards before returning to the hotel, but after that…

She'd worried he wouldn't wake up, that he wouldn't leave the ICU alive, but once he was here, she had assumed he was well on the road to recovery. That they were merely keeping him sedated to rest up. She shouldn't have buried her head in the ground. She shouldn't have avoided the doctors, shouldn't have ran from his side every damn day.

'However, the new antibiotics he's on, are the best we have, and the positives are he's breathing on his own, his blood pressure is stable, and his heart rate is good.'

'So, you're saying he's going to pull through this?' Victoria wanted to scoff. She'd heard all this before, many years ago.

'There are no guarantees in life,' Doctor Woods told her honestly. 'However, if he gets through the next few days, his prognosis is good.'

Victoria sensed there was a moment of hesitation, a *but* or a *however*, on this doctor's lips. 'Go on,' she prompted.

The other woman sighed. 'His femoral nerve was also nicked by the blade.'

Victoria frowned, she'd not done very well in school, only just scrapping by to gain her SEC from school. 'I don't know what that means.'

'There could be some permanent damage to his left leg—'

'He can't walk?' Victoria asked, her voice high with a hint of panic. Cormac was fiercely independent, he was not going to take that well, but they could easily make adaptions to the house to keep it that way. They could renovate the downstairs to be wheelchair-friendly, move their bedroom to the ground floor... They'd need a full bathroom adding, and a ramp to the entrance way. Or perhaps they could just install a life? They had pretty clever things nowadays to help with independent living.

'We'll have to wait until he wakes up to know if he'll be able to walk or if we can rehabilitate it. At the moment, we need to focus on him overcoming the infection and then we can deal with that.'

Victoria finally focused her attention on her motionless husband. 'What are his chances of fighting it off, of him waking up?'

'I'd say about eighty-twenty of him coming through this. If he hadn't lost so much blood, if we hadn't had to repair so much already, and if he hadn't already fought off one infection, we'd be in the high nineties. But we're still in a good place. Like I said, he's breathing for himself, and we're the ones keeping him sedated to help him.'

Victoria nodded. An eighty-percent chance. It was less than what her mother's doctors had told her.

'What do you think of the Royal Family?' Victoria asked, her eyes still fixed on Cormac's sleeping form.

'My lady?'

'Please, be honest.'

'Well, I'll be happier when your husband is out of here, preferably to go home,' she hastened to add. 'That way the trail of Royal Guards can disappear and I"ll be able to tend to my other patients again rather than just your husband.'

Victoria turned to her at that, brow raised in question.

'Oh, orders came down from on high *very* quickly. Your husband is to be my sole focus until he either recovers or...' She paused, her mouth pursed as she glanced towards Cormac's prone form. 'Lets just say, I hope he recovers—I like working here.'

Victoria nodded and turned back to Cormac.

Maybe, she could trust this doctor.

Maybe.

CHAPTER NINE

Victoria stared down at the landing floor, trying to see if she could find any traces of blood, but the image of Cormac lying there, bleeding out, with her hands desperately trying to stem the flow wouldn't stop coming to mind. How she'd sat there on her knees, crying and screaming for someone to help her; how Marcus had pulled her away from her husband's side as the paramedics rushed in. He'd gathered her in his arms, trying to comfort her, trying to get her to stop looking at the state Cormac was in, but she'd fought him, pleading with Cormac to hold on, to stay with her. She'd shouted at the crew, threatening them to save him else face her grandfather's wrath. She had no idea if that threat had been empty or not and she was glad she didn't have to find out.

The sound of soft footsteps nearby jarred her from her maudlin thoughts. She knew the staff were floating around, surreptitiously watching her to ensure she was okay, but it had been a hard three weeks and she was finding it more and more difficult to hold onto her composure as the days went by.

'Ma'am,' a gentle voice called from the bottom of the stairs.

'Yes, Chloe?' She quickly wiped at her eyes to get rid of the tears that clung to her lashes.

'Um.' The girl began to wring her hands and Victoria had to marvel at her bravery in speaking. She was the lowest on the ladder staffing wise, fresh out of training, and suffered with anxiety—which was why she'd not received any offers from royal households or so Kirstie had told her—so for her to speak up about something meant it was rather important.

'It's okay, Chloe, you can speak honestly,' she told the girl.

'It's nothing like that, ma'am, it's just, I don't want to add more pressure to you.'

Victoria held back the sigh that wanted to slip over her lips. 'Its fine,' she reassured the girl.

'It's Mr Belview.' The young maid bit her lip and glanced away before looking back at Victoria. 'He's, he said... He's not coming back, ma'am.' She said the last part in such a rush of breath, Victoria almost didn't catch it.

'I beg your pardon?' Chloe's face went white. 'No, no, I'm not blaming you. Did you say Belview isn't coming back?'

Chloe nodded, but said nothing more.

'Do you know why?'

The maid licked her lips, her eyes once again darting to the right, and Victoria understood this meant she was working up the courage to speak. She'd have to have a word with Ms Higgins, the housekeeper, about sending Chloe on such important missions. Start her off with simple stuff first, let her build up to announcements such as these.

'Apparently, he said he wasn't being paid enough to deal with attempted murders and break-ins. Said he was going back to a royal house where they'—she licked her lips again—'do things properly.'

'I see,' Victoria drawled. 'Very well, thank you for letting me know, Chloe.' The girl nodded and dipped into a little curtsey—that had to stop—before she scurried away.

Victoria slowly trudged down the stairs and headed towards her office. She grabbed her phone from the giant partner desk she had planned on sharing with Kirstie and sighed as she dropped into her chair; that was something else she needed to sort out. She called the administration department at the Grand Palace.

'Hello, Deborah, it's Victoria. I need a temporary PA. Yes, I know,' Victoria added, rolling her eyes as the woman on the line began to lament how awful it was about Kirstie's deception. 'I need someone who will be the picture of utmost discretion, who will know what I need before I need it, and who I won't even realise is here until I say their name.' She chuckled at Deborah's reply of *not much then*. 'Thank you, and—'

She stopped before she asked regarding the availability of a butler. It wouldn't look good to have to request two new members of staff on the same day. But more than that, she had a thought.

'Never mind. Yes, I look forward to meeting her.'

She quickly hung up and pressed the speed dial for the Penthouse number back in Avon. It rang a couple of times before Merryweather's cheerful, warm voice answered. He was surprised by her offer but promised to think it over and get back to her in the morning. She smiled as she hung up. He was an excellent butler, by far the best she'd ever had the pleasure of working with, even without royal training, and she desperately hoped he would take her up on her offer.

She spun the chair around and stared out through the large window towards the driveway. The wisteria that had decorated the bays was gone now, shrivelling up and dying in the milder weather that the winter season brought. Gosh she needed to get herself together, for herself more than anything. It was too easy for her to sit and mope now that James was back in school and she had too much time to herself.

She thought about going to the hospital again, but the idea twisted something inside her, pulling her in half as she battled with herself at the decision.

Her visits to Cormac had been difficult, seeing him lying there, unaware of her presence. She hadn't been able to stay for long, and each time she left, she felt she was abandoning him. Guilt ate away at her with each step she took from her husband and each minute she failed to return to his side. She was caught in limbo, unable to mourn him yet unable to celebrate his survival just in case it was short-lived. While Cormac's doctor seemed semi-trustworthy, in general Victoria didn't trust doctors. She hadn't since she was sixteen and they'd looked her straight in the eye, told her they were the best and her mother was in safe hands. Five months later, Mummy was gone.

Victoria had no idea how long she sat, staring at nothing and thinking the same, when the phone rang, jarring her from her solitude. She reached behind her, not wanting to ruin her staring contest with the tree line.

'Yes?' she answered without even checking the number. She expected Deborah to answer her, telling her when to expect her new secretary.

'*Lady Snape?*'

Victoria sighed. Every bloody time. 'It's Blake, but speaking.'

'*Apologies. It's Doctor Woods, I just wanted to give you a call and let you know that Mr Blake woke up a few minutes ago and—*'

Victoria sat up straight and let out a little bark of joy down the line, probably making the doctor recoil from the phone.

'He's awake? Really awake? Not like when they just open

their eyes on reflex?' she asked in a rush. Doctor Woods chuckled.

'*Trust me, he's* really *awake. He won't stop asking for you and James, demanding to know that you're okay and asking where you are. Ma'am, would you be so kind as to hurry down here so he can get some rest?*'

Victoria gave another peal of delighted laughter, imaging her husband giving the nurses hell, pressing his call button over and over until they took it away from him and refusing to return it until he behaved, which of course he wouldn't!

She couldn't help the girlish giggles that kept bubbling up, but she managed to tell the doctor she was on her way immediately before hanging up and running from the room.

'Where's Toby?' she shouted in the middle of the hallway, hoping one of her spying staff would respond.

'He's in the garage, my lady,' Chloe answered as she popped her head from a room that Victoria knew had been cleaned already at least three times that day. 'Is everything okay, ma'am?'

'He's awake, Chloe!' she cried, running over to the girl whose eyes opened wide in shock and horror as Victoria threw her arms around her. 'He's awake and asking for me!' She practically jumped up and down with the young maid as every part of her filled with joy and happiness, so much so she thought she might burst with it!

'I'm going there right now!' she told the girl. 'Well, I have to get James first.' Chloe nodded along, humouring her as her mouth ran a mile a minute. 'And I need to find Toby to take us! Oh, Chloe, I'm so happy!'

'Me too, ma'am,' she said with a forced smile. Victoria didn't care in that moment if she was making the girl uncomfortable, she was just too damn happy. She reached out and pinched the girl's cheeks as she laughed before she spun on her heel and bounced away to find Toby so she could go and see her husband again!

∼

She'd felt a moment of guilt when James shuffled into the headmaster's office, his head lowered, his shoulder hunched up as if he was waiting for the next blow. She'd cursed herself, realising she should have told the school the actual news, so he'd be greeted with a smile and a word of encouragement rather than allowing them all to think the worst. But she was so used to putting on her *public face,* she'd acted as if they didn't need to know.

'James,' she'd said, keeping her voice light. 'Cormac's awake, and he's asking to see you.'

Her young charge's head snapped up, his eyes wide with surprise before utter exaltation filled his hazel gaze. He squealed with happiness before running towards her and Victoria had just enough time to open her arms and scoop him up as he flung himself at her.

The staff, happy at the news, knowing how sad and withdrawn James had been over the past few days, waved them off with big smiles and well wishes.

Excitement filled them on the drive to the hospital, and they bounded out of the car with eager enthusiasm, James pulling her through the twisting and turning corridors towards Cormac's room as she hurried as quickly as she could behind him, trying not to topple in her heels.

'C'mon, Mum,' James said, tugging on her arm to try and get her to move quicker. Part of her heart jumped for joy at hearing herself referred to by such a title. She felt it a far greater honour to be worthy of such a title by this young child than any title her grandfather could bestow upon her. But the other part hammered in panic at his utterance; he wasn't supposed to be calling her that until Cormac said it was okay, and she *certainly* didn't want James saying it around him the moment they walked in the room. Cormac would be wondering what the hell she'd been doing in the time he'd been away, undermining his decisions, encouraging James to forget their parents.

'James.' She gently pulled on his hand until he slowed down again. 'Please don't call me that until Cormac says it's okay. Remember what we talked about?'

'But I want—'

'We don't want to make Cormac upset when he's *just* woken up, do we?' she interjected, slowly shaking her head to tell him the correct answer. Part of her laughed at her antics; the boy was far from stupid and James only confirmed such a thought when he rolled his eyes at her. Victoria briefly wondered what his teenage years were going to bring to them.

'Yeah, alright. Can we *go* now?' She laughed, dropping his hand as she quickly ran ahead, making him call out and give chase to her. Nurses and porters called out to them to *slow down* and *stop running!* but neither of them paid their spectators any heed as they ran full pelt to their destination.

'Ma'am?' one of the stationed Guards asked as she ran towards them, stumbling in her heels to stop.

'It's okay,' she panted, hands on her knees as she tried to catch her breath. 'Just a race with—*Umph!*'

James, in his jubilance, forgot how to apply the brakes. He crashed into Victoria, knocking her off her feet, and the two fell to the floor in a jumble of arms and legs, laughing and giggling the whole way down.

'Ugh, James!' she moaned as she lifted her head to peer at the boy who lay sprawled atop of her. 'You're getting heavy!'

'Am not!' he said with a little frown and a pout.

'Are too!' When his frown deepened, she bopped his nose with her finger and added, 'That means you're growing!'

His whole little face brightened at that comment; his size was a sore point for him, being the smallest of his peers.

'Do you really think?'

'Yes, now get off me!' she huffed, pushing at him. The other Guard, the one she recognised as Betts, reached down and hauled James up, setting him gently back on his feet. Now free, Victoria, with as much dignity as she could muster, climbed to her feet. She glanced at the unfamiliar Guard as she dusted herself off, ran her fingers through her hair, and smoothed the wrinkles out of her trousers. Betts scowled at the other man for not offering his hand, but rather than get into it, Victoria turned back to James.

'Okay, now when we go in, be sensible. No jumping on him, no tugging on his wires or tubes, no poking parts of him, or anything else like that, okay? He's going to be in a lot of pain.'

Pain because he'd thrown himself in front of her to take a knife she'd been told by doctors would have killed her if Cormac hadn't got in the way. You didn't do that for someone if you didn't love them; that was what each of her sisters had told her when she'd been unsure if his words were true.

She reminded herself of the only comment Hattie had made about the whole situation; *Actions speak louder than words.*

Of course, James didn't listen to her in the slightest and immediately pushed past her when she opened the door and rushed inside.

'Dad!' James shouted as he stopped for a second to check his brother was indeed in the bed, before he went on to charge again. Luckily, Victoria reached him just in time to stop him racing forward. She stood just inside the room, clasping James's shoulder gently in her hand as she held him back and gazed at her husband.

He looked as bad as the tea in this place. He was pale, his cheeks sunken, and despite being unconscious for weeks, he appeared exhausted. Big purple rings lined his eyes, his hair was dishevelled and in desperate need for a cut, and the tremendous number of pillows that propped him up and surrounded him made him look small and thin.

He was almost a different man.

'James! Victoria!' Cormac said when he opened his eyes to see the two of them standing there. His voice was rough from disuse and sounded weak and thready. 'I'm so glad you came.'

The relief of seeing him awake and staring at her with his green eyes, crinkled in the corner from a gentle smile, filled her body with relief and joy. She was glad she held onto James; she wobbled slightly as the strength went from her knees. Her charge stared up at her, his little face lined with worry as he suddenly realised his brother wasn't immediately back to the way he'd been before. She let go of her grip on James and gently nudged him towards Cormac, but James held back, his arm creeping around behind Victoria and clinging to her leg.

'Of course, we did,' she said, knowing what he meant, but not letting that get in the way of the moment. Yes, they'd have to talk, just to clear the air, but right now this was a moment of joy, of happiness. She gave Cormac a pointed look before dropping her gaze to James and then back to him, hoping he'd get the message that she wasn't doing *that* in front of his brother. 'Why wouldn't we?'

'Well, it's a school day, right? I'm sure the nurses said it was Wednesday.'

'It's *Thursday!*' James piped up, unwinding his arm and shuffling forward a little.

'It is indeed,' Victoria said as she moved around James and strode to the seat at the far side of Cormac's bed. 'I thought you finally joining us again in the land of the living was a good enough reason for James to miss this afternoon's classes. You're only missing PE, right?'

'And chess.' His voice dropped to a whisper as he took a step closer to the end of Cormac's bed.

'Merryweather knows how to play,' she said matter-of-factly. 'I'm sure he'll catch you up. How are you feeling?' she asked as she turned back to Cormac, but keeping a watchful eye on James in case he tried to play with one of the machines on the other side of the bed. 'Doctor Woods said you were causing hell.' She sighed and shook her head playfully. 'Really, Cormac?'

The blush that hit his cheeks made the rest of his skin look even whiter. He reminded her of the alcoholics she'd met at the rehab centre she'd opened a few years ago and just as she'd wanted to somehow fix all their problems, she wanted to fix his too. At least with Cormac, she had a real chance of doing that and not just throwing money at him. Although her mind did acknowledge the irony of *that* thought.

'Yeah,' he said a little bashfully. 'I just... I didn't know where I was when I woke up, and the last thing I remember is—'

'Falling down the stairs and cutting yourself on the vase you smashed?' she quickly interjected, her eyes sliding to James who had now made it as far as the middle of the bed. He stared intently at Cormac's hand where the cannula was taped to his skin.

'Yeah... That?' There was a question in his words and as she glanced towards him, his eyes held a hint of humour. She knew he was dying to say something like, *that's what you came up with?* and she carefully swatted at his free hand.

'You're still at the penthouse? You said Merryweather could teach James chess.'

'Yeah, we're still there,' James finally piped up with a sigh. 'Victoria said we can't move into the new house without you.'

'Yes,' Victoria added as she continued to watch James carefully even though she faced Cormac. His fingers were inching closer to Cormac's, and she didn't want him to mess with the cannula. 'The staff needed to fix the mess the vase left and what the paramedics did to get inside the house.'

'Ah, I see,' Cormac said, clearly understanding her hidden meaning. He went to say something more as Victoria saw James reach up for the cannula. His little fingers hovered just over it and she was about to bark out *no* when there was a rap on the door, startling them all. James snatched his hand back and did a full one-eighty turn on his feet, his face flushed and his eyes wide with guilt.

'Good afternoon! Sorry to interrupt,' Doctor Woods said cheerfully as she popped her head into the room. 'How are we all doing?'

'Very well, thank you,' Victoria said with a bright and warm smile. Despite her initial misgivings, the doctor had been wonderful, and she had nothing but respect for the woman who had turned that eighty-twenty ratio into one hundred-zero.

'Good-o! And what about you, young man?' Doctor Woods said, turning to James, whose eyes widened more. He quickly nodded before he dashed around the bed, giving the other woman as wide a berth as possible, and clambered onto Victoria's lap, burying his head into her chest.

'James?' Victoria said cautiously as she tried to pull away and see his face, but the boy clung tighter and refused to come out of his hiding place.

'Not to worry,' the other women said, her voice a little quieter, but no less cheerful by James' reaction. 'Perfectly normal for kids to freak out a little over the most mundane things during a difficult time like this.'

And what about adults? Victoria's mind asked, but she kept the question to herself.

'Now, Mr Blake, are you willing to listen to me?' Cormac's blush deepened, but he nodded. 'Okay, I won't overcomplicate things with lots of medical speak, I'll keep it nice and simple. The knife—'

'Vase!' Victoria quickly corrected the doctor as she tightened her hold on James. 'The vase that he knocked over when he fell down the stairs and landed on it.'

Doctor Woods' eyes glanced to James before flitting up to Victoria and eventually back to Cormac.

'Right. Yes, sorry. The *vase* cut through the abdominal muscles and punctured your lower intestine. We managed to close the puncture wound, but there may be some internal scarring from that. We should be on the lookout for things such as difficulty with bowel movements and so on, to ensure the tissue doesn't cause an obstruction in the future.

'You lost an awful lot of blood and we had to do several transfusions to save your life.'

'Wow, was it really that bad?' Cormac asked as he stared at the doctor with awe and horror and Victoria realised he hadn't actually considered the extent of his injuries. He'd just accepted he'd been stabbed and woken up in the hospital. She wasn't sure if that was a comfort or a worry that he took such a thing in his stride.

'Yes, Mr Blake.' Dr Woods, stared at him as if he had two heads. 'You almost died. Twice in fact.'

Victoria quickly cleared her throat again, glaring pointedly at the doctor as she cuddled James closer. The doctor looked a little annoyed that she had to keep correcting herself, and Victoria would have found it slightly amusing in other circumstances, but she didn't want James to even consider that there was a danger in his life at this age. If he did, his life would never go back to being the normal-ish one he'd had. She and her sisters had lost most of their childhood that way, and she wasn't about to risk his.

'After the surgery, and despite our best efforts, you did get a severe infection from the intestinal leak, which is why your recovery was slowed and your time in the ICU so long. Then, unfortunately, sepsis hit. Then there's the other issue...' Doctor Woods paused and glanced towards James again who was peeking back at her. 'The *vase* also nicked your femoral nerve. Now this is really unfortunate as this helps you walk and—'

'I can't walk?' Cormac asked, a hint of panic filling his voice, his head swiveling back and forth between Victoria and the doctor. Victoria leaned over and grasped his fingers, giving him silent support as Doctor Woods continued to explain. She'd tell him afterwards that she'd already had architects draw up plans for renovations if it came to that.

'Well, until we have you up and about, we're not sure of the extent of the problems the damage has caused. Now I want to stress that the nerve isn't completely severed, and we can repair it via surgery. I would recommend doing that as soon as possible.' She flicked back the bed covers to reveal his feet. 'If time wasn't of the essence with the other problems you'd had, we potentially could have done it when you came in, but we felt best to close you up and get you back on your feet, so to speak. Now, can you feel this?' she asked him as she pinched the big toe on his left foot.

'Yeah,' he said, a relieved smile on his face as he nodded. He tried to wiggle his toes, but the movement wasn't much, and the smile fell from his face.

'Okay, so there's some movement and sensation. If I pinch this one'—the doctor pinched his big toe on his right foot —'and then this one, which one do you feel more?'

'Definitely the right,' he said sullenly. 'I can feel the left, but it doesn't feel as if you're pressing on it as hard as the other.'

'Okay, we can work with that. As I said, surgery is your best option. You might not get complete feeling or one hundred percent movement back in it, but it should give you mobility again to live your life as you used to.' She paused. Glanced up at both of them before cheekily adding, 'Although you might not be able to do the splits anymore.'

'What?' Victoria asked, looking at Cormac whose cheeks were now flame red. 'You can do the splits?'

'Well, I *could*,' he muttered. 'I don't want to know how you know that.'

The doctor laughed heartily. 'It was my hen night back in February. We went to Avon for afternoon tea and fancy cocktails. What I didn't realise was said fancy cocktails would be at a place called *Monty's*.'

'Oh God!' Cormac covered his face with his hands as he shook his head in disbelief.

'Nothing to be bashful about—we had a whale of a time! We were very impressed with your flexibility. When your picture started to appear with Lady Snape all over the place, we weren't completely sure if you were the same guy we'd seen that night,' she continued on. 'But when *that* story came out, there was a lot of money changing hands between us girls.'

Victoria couldn't help it; she laughed at the idea of people who had been to see Cormac dancing, placing bets on if he was the new member of the Royal Family. How silly they were to think that no one would recognise him, but how amusing that people hadn't made a fuss, just quietly using it to have fun amongst themselves. It made her strangely proud of her nation.

'Which way did you bet?' she asked the other woman with a chuckle.

'Oh, I was pretty sure it was you.' Doctor Woods waggled her eyebrows at Cormac.

'Shit, I gave you a lap-dance, didn't I?' he groaned, rolling his head into the pillow to try and hide as much of his face as he could.

'I won the most money of everyone.'

Victoria howled with laughter, causing James to grab hold of her tighter in case she threw him off her knee.

'Fuck my life,' Cormac said.

'Language, Dad.' James turned his head to glare at Cormac. 'What's a lap-dance?'

The two women fell into hysterics as Cormac glared at the two of them.

'I hate you both. When's the surgery?'

The doctor took them through the process of the operation and the steps he'd need to take afterwards, and once they'd agreed on a date, when he was a little bit stronger, she left them to themselves.

James, from the safety of his seat on Victoria's knee, asked Cormac a lot of questions, such as did it still hurt and what did all the tubes do, which his brother answered as best he could. The atmosphere had been light and warm the whole time, and Victoria could almost forget they weren't in hospital, that they hadn't almost lost him, that they were simply at home, if it wasn't for the machines that still surrounded her husband. She also almost forgot they still had things they'd needed to discuss.

As she bent to press a kiss to his cheeks, she whispered, 'We still need to talk.'

'Yeah,' he said quietly as his gaze dropped to the crisp white bed linen.

'I'll come back and see you tomorrow, when James is in

school if you're up for it.' He nodded solemnly and Victoria almost wanted to tell him it was all going to be okay, just to take the weight from him. But she couldn't because she still wasn't sure how it was all going to play out.

She bent down and heaved James back up so he could lean over and give Cormac a hug goodbye.

'Get well soon,' James whispered.

Cormac nodded, his eyes welling up with tears, but he smiled through them, fighting them back, as he reached up and ruffled James' hair.

'Be good, buddy,' he said gruffly. 'Do whatever Victoria says, okay?'

'Dur,' James said, rolling his eyes and shaking his head. The laughter fell from Cormac's face as he glanced at Victoria.

'You raised him,' was all she said with a chuckle as she headed towards the door. 'Just think, he's still got his teenage years to go.'

She just managed to shut the door behind them as Cormac let out an expletive she hoped James didn't hear.

CHAPTER TEN

Victoria exited the car and ran towards the canopy over the entrance to the hospital, her shoes splashing in tiny puddles as she went. She shook her knee-length trench coat free of any excess water before she hurried through the automatic doors that slid open for her without a sound.

She followed the well-remembered pathway towards Cormac's room, but this time her feet were much slower and heavier than yesterday.

Yesterday, she'd been so excited and happy her husband had turned the final corner, that he'd finally woken up and was truly out of the woods. When she'd got home, she'd had a quick look online to see about the surgery and was pleased to see keyhole was an option, which meant a faster recovery time from the operation, although the nerve side of things would still take quite a while to heal. He would need physiotherapy for months or years. Possibly his whole life.

And then, after an animated dinner with James, reading him half a dozen stories in an attempt to get him to settle down and fall asleep, she'd been left alone. And that was when the thoughts returned, unbidden and unwanted. So, she'd done something she didn't do too often; she'd put the television on.

A romantic comedy was on the first channel and she quickly switched it over. It had taken some time to finally find something to keep her mind engaged, and she ended up falling asleep on the couch trying to work out who'd done 'it' in a dark thriller.

She'd dreamt of the night of the attack, of the voices in the shadows. Strangely, it hadn't been the violent rush of Ben Fuller charging at her or her hands uselessly trying to stop the blood that spilt from Cormac's stomach that had woken her in a cold sweat, but Cormac's voice pleading with her to listen to him, that he hadn't betrayed her, he wasn't a liar…

Had his deathbed confession been true? Had he meant his declarations of love or was that another lie? Something he needed to say to try and keep her and thus the lifestyle he had become accustomed to? Would she ever be able to believe him if he said they were true? Would she ever be able to trust him again?

She didn't want to spend her life second-guessing every word he said, questioning his every motive, wondering where he was really going when he went out or who he was speaking to on the phone. She didn't want to be one of *those* wives.

But the thoughts had lingered with her throughout the night, no matter how many times she'd tried to reason with herself that it was stupid. If she could listen to Kirstie and understand why she had fallen into the trap that O'Malley had lured her into, why couldn't she do the same with her husband?

It had been at dawn, as the beautiful orange sun slowly peeked over the horizon, when she'd realised her answer. Because she had so much more to lose with Cormac, the man she'd fallen in love with. If she accepted him back, if she forgave him, she was giving him her heart and was terrified that he'd break it.

That thought had lingered around her all morning, kept her quiet in the car with James as she dropped him at school, and slowed her steps to almost a stop as she turned the last corner and Cormac's door came into view at the far end of the corridor, the two assigned Guardsmen standing either side of it.

This wasn't how she should be feeling when being reunited with the man she loved, and resentment burnt away inside her over that, too. He'd saved her life, again, she should be dashing to him to be embraced in his strong arms, their kisses of reunion sweet and loving, hot and fiery…

This would have been so much easier if she hadn't fallen for him. Then she'd simply have been angry at Cormac for not telling her about O'Malley, and just as she had with Kirstie, they'd have dealt with it, putting tighter tabs on him until they had conceived. Then as soon as she'd given birth, he'd have been out of the door, paid in full, no returns, no refunds. But throwing love into the equation…

She had tried not to fall in love with him, not to hope that he would love her back, because it complicated their arrangement so much. Oh, she'd thought about it a lot in the beginning, and had even longed for the two of them to have the fairy tale ending, a story fit for the pages of a romance novel. But when she finally realised she *had* fallen for him, but hadn't seen evidence he felt the same, she'd tried to bury it deep within herself, to push it away, and to even try and stop loving him, knowing it was going to hurt so much when he walked away.

Loving him didn't just leave her bitter, it left her devastated. There wasn't just anger bubbling away, but disappointment, hurt… Would they ever be able to rebuild the trust between them? Would the relationship now be so damaged, they'd never get to truly experience what they'd stupidly denied themselves?

She should have been braver and just told him. Whispered the words one night after they'd made love. Taken the risk and experienced the feeling freely for as long as she could have until the world came crashing around her.

She ran her fingers through her hair, bringing her hands down around her neck and holding them there as she stared up at the ceiling, taking in one deep breath after another as she tried to stop her mind whirling with the self-destructive thoughts.

Cormac was alive and well and he'd said he loved her. Before she could decide anything else, she needed to know if that was the truth or not.

'Are you okay, Lady Blake?'

Victoria blinked, dropping her hands to her side as she stared dazedly at the Guard in front of her—the one who'd not offered his hand yesterday. He was so young, or perhaps she was just getting old?

'How old are you?' she heard the words before she realised she'd said them.

'Um, twenty-five, ma'am.' The poor guy looked completely perplexed by her random question.

The same age as Cormac, her brain taunted. He was so young, and she was so old. Why would he fall for someone so much older than him? He'd be able to go out and live his life —actually *have* a life—after their arrangement ended; she'd probably never marry again, but at least she'd have a child to love and cherish. Well, maybe.

'Ma'am? Do you want me to call for a doctor?' the Guardsman asked again. He glanced back over his shoulder where a nurse was coming along the corridor. He motioned towards the woman and Victoria quickly reached out to him, her hand gentle on his arm as she waved the nurse away with the other.

'I'm fine,' she told him with a wobbly smile. Dammit, why wasn't she able to slip into her public persona? Why was she letting everyone and their dog see her in such a state? The guardhouse was going to be rife with gossip this evening, meaning the maids would know of it shortly after, which would get back to the footmen, and then to Michael, the palace's head butler, who would tell Thomas, the King's private secretary, who, of course, would tell the King.

'It's just a difficult time,' she said, before looking pointedly towards the door he'd been stood before. 'Sometimes you just need to take a minute before you can gather enough courage to face down the world.'

The young Guard smiled and nodded his head as if he completely understood her words. She wished she did.

'Well, my husband's waiting. I hope he hasn't caused any trouble today?'

The man laughed. 'Not today, ma'am,' he said as he fell into step beside her. His actions made her raise a brow.

'How long have you been with the Royal Guard?'

The man blushed and dipped his head, and she couldn't help the smile that touched her lips; he reminded her of Cormac.

'Just graduated this week, ma'am!' he said, his chest puffing up with pride. 'This is my first assignment.'

Oh, he was so fresh and green, she couldn't do it, she couldn't tell him not to walk at her side as if they were old friends, that he was supposed to be two steps behind her, silent, save for instructions in case anyone came at them. But if she didn't tell him, she was sure one of her damn cousins would on his next assignment, and not be in any way kind.

'What's your name?' she asked as they stopped outside Cormac's door. She turned to face him properly.

'David. David Kenner.' He beamed at her proudly as he stuck out his hand.

'Well, David Kenner, I'm sure you're going to have a long and illustrious career,' she said as she carefully shook his hand. 'And I'm sure that Officer Betts here will be sure to give you some careful, and *polite* feedback on your kind actions to me today.'

She looked at the aging Guard who had accompanied her a few times over the years as she turned to go into Cormac's room. Her look said *be nice* and the eye-roll she got back made her bite her lip to stop laughing. He always complained he got stuck with the newbies and Marcus said he assigned them to him *because* he complained. But he was also brilliant at turning them into outstanding officers. David Kenner must be a promising recruit.

She pushed the door handle down and walked in with her head held high.

'Well, you look happier than I thought you would,' Cormac said from his bed, one brow raised in question. He was trying to exude an air of confidence, but the way his fingers played with the hem of the blankets told a different story. He was as nervous as she was and suddenly, that made her feel a bit better. He clearly wasn't the mastermind liar she'd been considering him to be.

Victoria swallowed the sickly feeling that had risen from her stomach and offered him the barest hint of a smile.

'How did you expect me to be?' her voice was quiet, far shyer than she'd meant.

'I wasn't sure if Mr Daven would be accompanying you,' he said with a nervous laugh. Her eyes went wide at the suggestion. She'd never actually considered that; was that really what he thought of her?

And why not? her brain piped up again. *That's exactly who you took him to when you wanted to nail him down for marriage.*

If you were to cast him aside, Mr Daven would probably be who you'd go to.

'I'm not looking to divorce you, Cormac.' Frowning, she stepped slowly around his bed, heading for the chair. 'Well, at least not now. That probably depends upon how this turns out.'

He swallowed at her words.

'What I am wanting to do is to talk about what happened that night and why it happened in the first place.'

Her husband sighed and dropped the bedding from between his fingers as he sat back against the pillows. He simply stared at her, his eyes searching hers, but for what, she didn't know. Was he trying to figure out the best way to play her? Was he looking for just a hint that she might forgive him and accept his heart the way she wanted him to accept hers?

Why weren't her mother's words true; why couldn't everything be solved with a good cup of tea?

'What do you want to ask?'

'Were you part of Simon's plan the night we first met?'

'God, no!' He looked horrified and disgusted at the suggestion, and Victoria knew immediately he was speaking the truth. It was a mean thing to do, knowing full well that Simon hadn't had a clue who Cormac was—no television or newspapers at the Hill for him to keep up on the royal romance. But she needed to get him speaking the truth so she could see when he'd begun to lie—*if* he'd lied.

'So, our first meeting was completely by happenstance?'

'I guess so,' he said, but he sounded hesitant. 'I mean... unless Simon chased you there?'

Was he trying to figure if O'Malley had set them up to meet? It wasn't beyond the realm of possibility, but Victoria didn't think that was the case. She shook her head. 'I led the way.'

'Then I couldn't have been part of it.'

'I suppose not. So...' She took a deep breath. 'Just when *did* you get involved with it? And I'm not talking about when you picked me up off the tarmac that night.'

So he told her the story of how O'Malley had interrupted his dance practice, what he had offered, and how the man had spoken about Victoria. He also reiterated that he *had* turned it down. Initially.

'I cracked when I got home,' he confessed. 'It didn't really seem real when I was getting dressed afterwards, and I barely remember the drive home; my mind was just a blank. But when I reached my door and I realised my little brother was waiting for me, that I had so many bills to pay...' He glanced down guiltily at the bedcovers.

'You decided to accept his deal?'

'No.' His voice was small, high, and quiet, almost like he was a child in trouble. 'I considered if I should give James up to the boarding homes. Find him a *real* family, with a mum and dad someplace nice and safe.'

'Oh.' If it were anatomically possible, she would have sworn she felt her heart ache for him.

'And then when I saw James just sleeping there so quietly—'

'He was asleep? When you had practice?' That was weird. Surely, practice was in the day?

'The club closes Sunday to Tuesday. The clientele apparently wasn't that great, and it was costing more to keep it open those nights *and* have us in during the day to rehearse. Sunday night off, Mondays and Tuesdays for rehearsal.' He shrugged. 'At least that's what the boys told me when I started—was a genius move by *Britney*'—he spat the woman's name out—'when she took over the club.'

'You don't like this Britney, I guess?'

'Seriously? Victoria, she was one of those there that night, at the bottom of the stairs.'

'She was?' He nodded and a flash of memory came back to her... *If O'Malley could get the Head of the Guard...* 'That was *her*?' Another nod. Victoria slumped back into her chair. 'Wow. O'Malley really has his fingers in everyone, doesn't he?'

'From what I gather.'

'I'm sorry,' she said, sitting back up. 'I interrupted. You were saying that you went in and saw James...'

And so, he told her about changing his mind, about not being able to give his brother up, and he went and made the call to O'Malley saying he'd do it.

'He didn't honour the original deal, of course, but he cleared off the rent arrears. That was all I cared about really. I could manage the rest after that.'

'So, your boss didn't reward you for rescuing me, it was a payment for giving away my secret?'

He was back to staring at the bed again, his shoulders hunched and his fingers twisted in the bedsheets.

It looked so strange, a man of his stature trying to shrink into nothing. Her father would probably have laughed, would have told him to *man up*, that men took their errors and played them into strengths. Turned them on the person they'd wronged until they thought that *they* were the ones who'd made the mistake. She'd had a similar spiel thrown at her a few times after her mother had passed.

But right now, hunched up and looking so sorrowful, Cormac looked more a man than any other in the world. He was owning his mistakes, accepting them, willing to take whatever the consequences were. He wasn't hiding, wasn't trying to twist anything, and that was when it hit Victoria.

She was going to fight for him. She wanted to love him and for him to love her in return. She wanted to trust him, to be with him, to spend the rest of her life with him at her side. She wanted to share laughter with him, lazy mornings in bed entangled with him, and many more meals that ended with the two of them entwined in passion.

She wanted a life with him.

'Yeah,' he said quietly. Then something seemed to strike him. 'No... I dunno. He said it was for rescuing you, but it was probably just a payment so he had something to blackmail me with later. Probably would have kept me under this thumb even if I had told him the truth about why you'd wanted to see me.'

And after what Kirstie had told her, Victoria knew that to be the truth. What a feather in O'Malley's cap it would have been to get someone beholden to him in not only the Snape household, but the royal one too. But there was a more pressing matter she wanted to get to, a question she'd been dying to ask the moment she walked in.

'And why didn't you tell me about O'Malley? I could have helped.'

He sighed as he rubbed his hands over his face before he ran his fingers through his hair.

'Well, I...' he trailed off and stared across the room. She could see his mind working a mile a minute trying to figure out what to say. She narrowed her eyes as she tried to fathom if he was looking for the right lie to tell her or simply working out the best way to say his answer.

'I just thought you'd tell me to go.' The answer was simple and straight to the point. 'And I suddenly had a way out of all the money problems I had. James would have opportunities even *I* hadn't had as a kid. I wanted him safe and fed and... and...'

'And?' she prompted.

'And... I wanted the chance too. You were offering me the world on a platter and if I told you about O'Malley and you took it away... I don't think I could have survived afterwards.' There was a slight hitch to his voice as he finally admitted—probably to himself for the first time—what this meant to him, and Victoria couldn't take it any longer.

She reached out, took his hand in hers and squeezed it. Both his hands grabbed at her, holding onto her own like it was a lifeline; a rope pulling him from whatever deep, dark pit he'd probably been living in since he'd woken, wondering what the hell was going to happen to him now. It hurt her to think of him feeling that way, of suffering and her vision swam with tears.

'I just need to know one more thing,' she said, her voice shaking. He glanced up at her, his green eyes ringed with red as the tears slowly tracked their way down his face. He swallowed and nodded, trying to be brave and ready for whatever she was about to throw at him.

'That night, you said... you said you loved me. Was that the truth or were you just—'

He pulled her to him, wrapping her in his arms and crushing her lips against his own. She clung to him for dear life as he kissed her with a desperation, a *need* for her to feel his passion, his emotions... his love.

She kissed him back, pouring everything of her own into it, wanting him to know how much he filled her heart, touched her soul, completed her in all the corny ways the women in Alexi's trashy romance novels said their heroes did. And Cormac was her hero in every sense of the word.

He pulled back, pressing his forehead to hers as he dragged in ragged breath after ragged breath, possibly trying to calm his racing heart that beat where her hand had fallen against his bare chest. Her own was pitter-pattering at a similar rate.

'I love you, Victoria Georgina Blake, with everything that I have. If you told me to leave you and never return, I would, simply because you asked, but it wouldn't stop me from loving you. I hope you don't ask though, because I want to spend every day for the rest of my life showing you how much you mean to me, how much my heart is completely yours.'

'Oh, Cormac,' she sighed. 'I love you too, totally and utterly,' she murmured against his lips and his arms tightened around her.

'I am *never* letting you go,' he told her, and she hoped he never did.

CHAPTER ELEVEN

It had been a difficult few weeks for Victoria, dealing with the fall-out of Kirstie's betrayal. Marcus had spoken to Cormac about Britney, the suspect that was still missing. She was quickly rounded up and dispatched to the Broken Hill, cursing her former employee the whole way, or so Victoria had been told.

Marcus had the unfortunate job of letting her know none of them were giving up O'Malley. It transpired that Ben Fuller had been brought in for one reason and one reason only—to be the fall guy for the whole thing.

Victoria felt a little sorry for the man. His doctors had told them that when he'd been released from their care, he'd been doing very well; he had clear lines between reality and fantasy and had several coping strategies to help him. They'd had high hopes he would have some form of a future. But from what Marcus could get from Ben now, it appeared that he'd been targeted by O'Malley almost immediately.

The bastard had filled his brain with confusion and doubt. Apparently, it hadn't taken much to blur those lines again, as O'Malley fed Ben lie after lie of how Victoria was cheating on him with Cormac. Ben had fallen nicely into the trap, and with his current mental state the way it was, he couldn't be sure if the man who'd told him such things had really been there or if he was merely a figment of his own imagination.

She had broken her rule a second time and had witnessed his interrogation at the Hill and after seeing him so hopeless and pathetic, scared out of his wits by being in such a place, she'd once more given her grace, requesting he be moved to a secure psychiatric facility for life rather than imprisoned. She felt it just, and they'd agreed.

And with all the racing between Avon, the house, Highbourne, and Earlsbury General, she was feeling rather frazzled and at the point where something had to give when Doctor Woods had called her to say that Cormac could come home. And now, finally, that day was here.

Her husband carefully eased himself out of the car as she raced around from the other side, dithering on the spot, unsure if she should offer him help or let him do it on his own.

'Calm down, woman,' he said with a good-natured grumble. 'I got this.' And he did.

'Dad, you *have* to use this! The doctor said so,' James called out, almost falling from the back of the car after Cormac as he wielded the far too large cane. Victoria bit back the smile, dipping her head and turning away slightly so her husband wouldn't see her amusement as he rolled his eyes to the heavens.

'I'm not old enough for one of these things,' he said to her as he took it from James' outstretched hands.

'Oh, shush,' she chided as he stepped towards her. He'd probably have the limp for the rest of his life, but at least he had his *life,* as she kept pointing out whenever he mentioned it. 'Besides, I think it makes you look very distinguished,' she added, looking up at him coyly. 'Very lord of the manor.'

'I'll give you, *lord of the manor*,' he said gruffly into her ear with all the promise of things to come later that night.

'Are you a lord now?' James asked with wide open eyes.

'No,' Victoria told the boy, laughing.

'I wouldn't accept it,' Cormac said matter of factly.

'About that.' Victoria bit her lip and looked up at him through her lashes. 'Grandfather wants to see you. Said something about being rewarded for your heroic deeds.' Her husband groaned.

'I don't want a reward. I don't *need* a reward. I didn't do it for that.'

'I know,' she said, trying to placate him. 'I know, but it's the King's will.'

He made a dissatisfied grunting noise before he took a deep breath and turned to James with a smile.

'Now, *Son*.'

James' little mouth fell open and mirrored Victoria's own surprise at the use of the word *son*. In all the time James had been calling Cormac *Dad*, never had Cormac identified James as anything other than James, buddy, dude or something similar.

But he wasn't finished.

'Pick that jaw up off the floor'—he popped his finger under James' chin and gently closed his mouth—'and help your mum get me into the house.'

The smile that burst across James' face could have lit up the whole sky.

'Yes, Dad! C'mon, *Mum!*' he shouted as he quickly pushed his way between them and grabbed their hands in each of his.

Victoria gave Cormac a curious stare as he leaned across James to press a kiss to her stunned lips.

'Well, I've been told that a good lord of the manor should have a family. What do you say?'

'I say, we need to make it bigger.'

'I have a few ideas on that,' he murmured before he kissed her.

THE END

BEATING THE SYSTEM SAMPLE

CHAPTER 1 SAMPLE OF BEATING THE SYSTEM

Available NOW

Lady Henrietta Constantine Snape, twenty-fifth in line for the Crown of Avalone, swirled her drink with her straw as she stared at the twisting oranges, reds, and yellows of the juices that did nothing to hide the liberal quantities of alcohol the bar owner had poured into the bottom of her glass.

Flicking her finger at the paper umbrella, she scowled at the wasted pieces of fruit mixed between the ice. Although the juices in the drink were also a waste; they were slowing down her quest to get a nice fuzzy feeling to forget all about her sisters and their problems.

Bitches wouldn't know a *real* problem if it slapped them in the face. Alexandra wanting to be a queen—although Hattie wasn't sure she didn't already have something up her sleeve from the way she spoke at Victoria's wedding—

Philippa worrying over her business, the most successful accountancy firm in the country, and Victoria... Yeah, okay Victoria had problems with Cormac almost being killed at Christmas. But she needed to stop stressing about the lack of a baby.

She rolled her eyes at herself in the mirror over the bar. Perfect bloody Victoria. Somehow she'd managed to find a great guy in the weirdest of circumstances, *paying* him to marry her, and then falling totally and utterly in love with him. And he with her! But it wasn't enough, the baby that would ensure Victoria control over her share of their inheritance was eluding them. Why she was fretting, Hattie didn't know. After all, things always seemed to work out for Victoria. She'd have a baby in no time if she just stopped thinking about it.

Well, that and telling her three sisters to hurry up about getting their own inheritance sorted. Hattie wasn't bothered; no, she didn't want the money being bestowed on her grandfather—something her father had put in to encourage them all up the aisle, she'd bet—but she didn't *need* the money. When she worked, she was well paid. She owned her home outright, and she had no plans of ever having children. There wasn't a deep-seated need within her to start a family; the mere idea of wiping a kid's nose—or worse, an arse!—churned her stomach, and the thought of something latching on to her breasts to be fed—

Her hand flew to her mouth automatically as her body threatened to vomit over the shiny bar.

'Everything okay with your drink, my lady?' the far handsomer and much younger bartender asked as he wiped down the counter with a cloth. She forced a smile to her lips, before wrapping them around the straw and sucking, long and slow. The man's eyes dropped to watch, and she ensured she caught the last drop off the straw with her tongue before she sat back.

'Perfect,' she purred. She wouldn't mind *him* sucking her breasts. The bartender made to say something in return when someone jumped up on the stool next to her.

'Fancy meeting you here,' a familiar, deep voice rumbled in her ear.

'Back in town, Jensen?' she said, turning her barstool to face the new arrival. She cocked her head to one side; the suit was certainly a new look for her beach loving friend, whose usual attire consisted of flip-flops and shorts. His calves were probably wondering why the hell they were covered for the first time in over a decade.

'How'd you know it was me? Everyone else thought I was Roman,' he said with a pout as she met his amber eyes. Sighing, she raised her brows, silently asking him to get real. 'Ah, I should've known I'd never be able to fool you.' He shifted on his stool to face the bar and waved for the young bartender he'd chased off to come back. 'You love my brother too much to ever believe I was him.'

It may have been years since her young heart had been given to the man who looked identical to the one who sat next to her, but still; just the idea of Roman Tyrrell quickened her pulse and stole her breath. The way he smiled at her, the secretive grin he kept just for when they were alone, or the deep timbre of his voice as he murmured his hopes and dreams in her ear...

'I don't *love* Roman,' she protested, a little too quickly even for her own ears.

'Hattie, c'mon—whisky neat,' he told the other man before facing her again. 'You were his little shadow; wherever my brother went, you were right there with him.'

'He was my friend nothing more,' she lied. As she took another long pull of her drink, she pretended not to picture the identical, yet—at least in her eyes—very different face of Jensen's twin brother. Finishing her fruity concoction off far quicker than she really should have, she motioned to the bar's owner with her finger that she wanted another.

'We never understood it,' Jensen said, his voice low, as he stared down at the wood of the counter, his fingers tracing the grain of the wood. 'How he never fell in love with you the way you loved him.' She made to protest, but Jensen's hand closed over hers, silencing her before she could speak. 'Don't deny it, we all saw it. He was *it* for you, and what he did was a dick move.'

Hattie rolled her head back as she made an *ugh* sound. Sure, Roman had stolen her heart, but he hadn't loved her back. She didn't hold *that* against him, even if she did lament it.

'All he did was back his girlfriend,' she said firmly, nodding her thanks to the owner as he put their drinks in front of them. She waited for the man to walk away before huffing in irritation as she removed the decorations around the top of the cocktail *again*. 'Who had every right to defend her relationship, no matter how wrong she was.'

Liar.

'It was, what?' she asked, fingers reaching inside the glass to pluck out an orange slice. 'Fifteen-ish years ago? He's still with her, they must be very happy together'— Jensen snorted—'and I wish them all the best. I don't hold grudges.'

Stop telling porkies...

'Fiona'—Jensen's upper lip curled up in disgust at saying the name of his soon to be sister-in-law—'was and still *is* a cow. He should have put her in her place when she accused you of being a stalker, sorry a *bloody bunny boiler*, not *sided* with her. And certainly not in front of all of us.' Jensen raised his glass to her before downing it in one. He held the tumbler back out to the nearest barman and ordered the same again. Hattie frowned at the action.

Jensen was never a spirit drinker, always a beer kind of guy, he'd nurse one for hours before someone would take it off him and replace it with another; fresh and cooler.

'It was like he had forgotten all about the four years he'd spent with you because he was suddenly getting his leg over. It was just so *unlike* Roman. I mean give him his due, he's an absolute bastard in every aspect of his life, but until that moment he'd always been loyal to his friends.'

'Look,' she snapped, irritation bubbling up. Why couldn't she ever just have a nice quiet drink? 'I don't know why Roman never returned my feelings. I don't know what he sees in Fiona or why he fell for her and not me, but I do know that I wasn't a guaranteed lay. Maybe she was, and that's what he wanted.'

Liar, liar pants on fire!

Jensen threw his head back and roared with laughter. The barman she'd been hoping would take her into the back room during his next break, eyed her friend as he delivered his second drink.

Elbows up on the bar and chin in her hand, she watched the hot, young bartender go on his break, glancing over to her as he slowly closed the door to the stock room behind him. Hattie sighed.

She *had* been a sure thing. So sure, she'd spread her legs for Roman the first chance she'd got. It had been their last Christmas at Guildford University, and Jensen had brought them drinks from the student union. She'd had a sip of one of the beers and found it disgusting and pushed it back at Jensen, saying *no, thank you*. They'd all laughed at her, told her she was still a baby.

Sweet sixteen and never been kissed, they'd all teased, and while she'd laughed it off with them, Roman—who had flat out refused the beers from the start, calling them vile—had later found her hiding in her suite, desperately trying to stop the tears that fell.

How was she supposed to get kissed? She was only sixteen and stuck at university! *Men* filled the hallways and lecture theatres. She might have the mental capacity and work ethic akin to her professors, but everyone saw her as a child. Even *he* saw her as such, she'd accused in her ire.

No, never. He'd said it with such conviction, such truth, she'd felt it in her heart. He'd shook his head while holding her gaze; his warm whisky eyes filled with a fire, a surety she'd never seen in anyone before or since, and it had taken her breath away as he'd lowered his head to hers.

Their lips met, and she gave him her first kiss; an hour later, her virginity.

The following morning she'd woken up slightly sore but deeply satisfied and wholly content as she snuggled deeper into his arms. She felt she was exactly where she was supposed to be, that perhaps everything she'd endured in her short life was to lead her to him, to be in that moment, wrapped in his embrace. But the universe wasn't that kind to her.

She remembered every word he'd thrown at her after he'd woken up and realised he'd cheated on his girlfriend. How Roman had accused her of tricking him into her bed, trying to get her twisted, infatuated claws into him in an attempt to snatch him from Fiona. She couldn't stand that *he* had someone and she didn't.

That someone else had taken his heart.

She also vividly recalled how he'd threatened her, that if she ever spoke of what had happened between them to *anyone*, she'd be sorry.

She'd spent so long trying to work out what she'd done to *make* him fall into bed with her; it had taken years before she'd understood that he'd been eighteen, filled with hormones, and that even the sensible, level-headed, overly serious Roman Tyrrell could be controlled by his penis for a few minutes. Everything he'd said had merely been manspeak for *I've colossally screwed up and I'm going to use* you *as a means to get out of the blame.*

She should have told Fiona. Perhaps if she had, the poor woman might have found a man to give her the solid gold ring to match the diamond Roman had finally given her at Christmas—although no official announcement had followed. But Fiona's perseverance had finally paid off; maybe in another fifteen years she'd finally get to say *I do*.

'So, what's with the get up?' Hattie asked, peering at Jensen through her lashes as she took another sip of her drink. He downed his immediately. She pursed her lips together to stop herself from berating him when he asked for a third and settled on saying, 'Did you suddenly grow up?'

'How very dare you!' he said in mock outrage, slamming his once again empty glass on the counter. 'I will never grow up. *Never!*' Hattie couldn't help the small giggle that bubbled from her lips. *That* was the Jensen they all knew and loved; always the class clown, the fun one of their small group.

'So?' she prompted.

'So, I'm playing a game.'

'Oh, no.' She quickly pushed her glass across the bar and grabbed her bag ready to leave, her sobriety immediately returning. 'I'm not getting involved in another one of your *games,*' she told him as she spun away from her guest. The last time they'd played a game had been three years ago when she'd ended up practically naked in the middle of London with no passport, no money, and a bleary memory of how she'd even got there in the first place.

Her father had gone ballistic when she'd called home asking for help, promptly forbidding her from ever seeing

Jensen or their small group of friends again. She'd promised him, but reneged on it a few months later when Jensen and a couple of others had rolled back into her part of Avalone. While they hadn't played any *games*, her father had found out and kept his word—he'd refused to speak to her.

Okay, *that* she definitely held a grudge for. Her father should have accepted her calls, especially when he knew he was ill. He was the parent. He should have realised that children, no matter how old, made mistakes and needed their mothers and fathers to turn to. He'd abandoned her. Left her alone and pointedly ignored her until she'd eventually given up... Only two months before his death.

The bastard.

'Hattie.' Jensen's hand closed over her own, as she'd braced it against the bar to jump down from the stool. 'Please don't go.' She glanced at him over her shoulder, freezing at the look of loss, hurt, helplessness, and a myriad of other emotions on his face. She saw so much pain and sadness in his being, that Hattie wondered how anyone could feel so much and still be standing.

'Jensen, what's happened?' she asked, but the moment the words were out of her mouth, his serious demeanour changed, and the smile was back on his lips. However, this time she noticed the usual playfulness he exuded didn't reach his eyes; eyes usually so open and warm no matter what, were now closed and empty. He turned back to the bar and waved his empty glass at the bar's owner, ignoring her question.

'Jensen?' She twisted her hand in his and grasped at it, surprised when he clung back so fiercely, as if it were a lifeline for a man cast away into the tumultuous ocean, but he didn't turn to face her.

'Not here,' he told her, releasing her hand and knocking

back the drink the barman put in front of him. 'I- I've got a car—you're not far from here, right?'

'It's walkable,' she told him, not liking the idea of either of them behind the wheel that night. 'And the sand beneath our feet will be nice.'

He nodded, rubbing his hands on his trousers nervously, before glancing down at his leather covered feet with another frown.

They left the bar in silence, a far cry from the way they'd left such establishments in the past. A night out with Jensen was always something to remember, always a time she ended up doing something she'd never have done without him there, giving her the confidence, cheering her on… She had so many good memories with the man at her side. Yet, she realised as they stopped to remove their shoes at the edge of the sandy beach that lined miles of the north eastern shores of Avalone, she'd never been out alone with Jensen before. They'd always been in a group.

Roman, Jensen, Constance, Fiona, Julia, Ben, Heidi, Freddie and little Hattie, the brainiacs sent off to the Guildford University Gifted Programme. And oh, how they'd clung together, even after they'd graduated.

They'd been peerless; too young for university life, too smart to attend an academy. None of them had friends their own age, save for their small clique. It had been worse for her; she'd been almost two years younger than the rest of them, just turned thirteen-years-old. The soil on her mother's grave not even settled before she'd been torn from her sisters and packed off across the country. She wasn't the only one with a tale to tell, but hers was by far the most obvious and rawest.

The girls had become her surrogate sisters, while the boys became her annoying brothers—something she'd relished.

Finally, something just for her, something Victoria, Pippa, and Alexi would never know.

Roman never fell into the *brother* category. From the moment she'd met him she'd been lost to his good looks; his rich, amber eyes seeming to see right through her, touched her in a way no other ever had or been able to since.

Of course, as soon as Jensen discovered her crush on his brother, he'd tried to impersonate Roman multiple times to catch her out. But while he could fool almost everyone else, his eyes weren't Roman's. She always knew.

'Seriously,' she said after Jensen tucked his phone away after sending a message to someone. 'Why are you dressed like Roman? I thought you'd given up pretending to be him.'

Jensen shrugged his shoulders, staring out across the dark ocean only illuminated by the low-hanging, full moon. The crests of the waves, bright white in the moon's light, rose and fell, crashing over the shoreline, threatening to tickle their feet as they went.

'Do you ever wish you could just…' He sighed and bent low to pick up a dazzling white shell half buried in the sand. He dropped his shoes and kept his eyes on his prize as he brushed the sand away, running his finger over the curves and curls, before throwing it back into the ocean. 'Do you ever wish you weren't part of the royal family or a Snape? That you'd not been smarter than everyone else and just been able to go to an academy like the rest of the country, instead of earning your degrees at sixteen?'

Her bottom lip rolled between her teeth as she listened to his words, trying to work out what he wasn't saying. Something big had happened, and he was desperately unhappy about it. However, the problem with Jensen was that for all the talking he did, he never knew how to discuss the important stuff.

'I suppose it would have been nice to have had more

friends,' Hattie said, honestly. 'But then, having my PhD by nineteen was rather nice too.'

'But the rest?'

She sighed as she pointed him towards her house, and they turned to head towards it. It was small, far smaller than he probably expected, and while she could have afforded much bigger, she'd immediately fallen in love with its cute exterior and the intimate space inside.

'I suppose it would have meant a different way of life not being in my family—in both aspects. Although it can be infuriatingly annoying, being the granddaughter of the King, it hasn't really hindered me in any way, not the way Victoria has suffered for it.' She shrugged. 'It certainly opened plenty of doors for me without me even needing to ask.'

'So, you wouldn't change that, but what about being a Snape?'

Hattie ground her teeth at the thought of her father and how much he'd changed after her mother had passed away. He'd become cold, distant; focused too much on his business and never on them. Hell, *he'd* been the one to send her on the gifted programme just weeks after his wife's death. Her mother hadn't wanted her to go and had she not died, Melinda would never have allowed it—not at just thirteen-years-old.

But if she hadn't gone, she'd have never met Roman, Jensen, or any of her other friends. And for as much as Roman had hurt her in the end, for most of those four years he'd been a friend to her the way no other ever had. Not even Jensen.

'No,' Hattie finally said as they reached the back of her beach cottage. The little decked balcony that overlooked the sandy shore wasn't very big and standing next to Jensen, who was as broad as he was tall, it felt even smaller. She opened the door and stepped inside, Jensen slowly following. He stood in the doorway, fidgeting with the buttons on his jacket until she flicked on the table light.

'Cosy.'

'It does me,' she said, falling onto the overstuffed couch. She smiled up at him and patted the seat next to her. 'I love it here. It's calm, out of the way, so peaceful. I barely see my neighbours because they're all second homes... And it's not as if any of my cousins are going to rock up to a place like this.' She snorted at the thought of one of the royal cars pulling up in front of the colourful row of tiny beach cottages.

'I don't think I'll ever get my head around your mother being a princess and that your grandfather is the freaking King. Doesn't seem real with you being... Well, you.'

'It's all overrated,' she said with a sigh. 'I mean it's not so bad for Pippa, Alexi, and myself, but for Victoria it can be a bit of a nightmare. *The Lady Blake*, la-de-dah. You couldn't pay me to do it.' Hattie rested her head back against the sofa to stare up at the ceiling. 'What about you?' she asked before he could say anything about Victoria. 'You wish you weren't a Tyrrell? Or clever? Or a twin?' She turned her head to face him at the last question. 'Can't imagine that's easy.'

'D'you know that when Roman and I did our entry tests for the programme, I scored eleven points more than him? I was only five behind you.' He raised a brow in a perfect arch the way she'd never been able to do. She stared at it for a second before meeting his eyes again. While Roman's eyes had always seared her soul, Jensen's filled her with warmth. They brought a smile to her face even when she didn't want them to.

'So, if you're the smarter twin, why aren't *you* vice president of your father's company?'

It was Jensen's turn to snort. 'That would mean I'd have to wear getups like this'—he waved his hand at his outfit—'all the time. No thanks.' He shook his head and turned his attention to the room. His eyes landed on the table next to him and the radio that took pride of place there. He pressed the *on* button and the smooth voice of the late-night radio host filled the room, announcing the next song.

'Dance with me,' Jensen said, turning back to her and holding out his hand. She shook her head but smiled as she put her hand in his, allowing him to pull her from the couch as he stood. His arms wrapped around her waist and gathered her against his body, nestling her in a cocoon of warmth. They moved together slowly, their bodies swaying as one, while Billy Paul's "Me and Mrs Jones" swirled around them.

'What happened with you and Roman?' he murmured into her hair. 'For years it was almost like *you* were his twin and then one day you and Fiona are screaming at each other and he... Well, you know better than anyone. The truth, Hattie. Please?'

She shifted, not leaving his embrace but drew back slightly so she could meet his gaze. Perhaps, if she hadn't met Roman first, maybe if Jensen had been the one to see her that first night, curled up on her duvet, shivering and shaking with sobs, not understanding why she'd been sent away, why her mother had died, and why her father no longer wanted her, he'd have been the one to capture her heart. But it had been Roman who'd walked past her room that night and heard her heartbreak. Roman who had wrapped his arms around her and given her a shoulder to cry on, who'd told her he'd watch out for her and promised she wouldn't be alone...

'We slept together.' The words fell out of her mouth, surprising even her. She opened her mouth to try and take them back, but Jensen was already nodding.

'I see.' He said the words slowly, and she couldn't work

out if the news was a surprise or not. 'We *all* suspected, but neither of you said anything.'

'He hated me afterwards.' She ducked her head, feeling that same shame she had all those years ago, one she just couldn't grow out of. 'He said I cornered him. That I *made* him cheat on Fiona and that—'

'The bastard,' Jensen muttered the curse, making her look back up. 'Their whole relationship is based around their names,' he told her with a shake of his head. 'You keep saying they must be happy together, but they don't love each other. *They see other people all the time*; it's just a match made on paper. Good business sense. She's the heir to the Martin line, and Roman…Well, I'm sure father has already made it so that Roman inherits everything on our side.'

Hattie blinked at the revelation. 'What?' she whispered.

'I mean,' he said, stopping their slow dance, his brows furrowed as he thought. 'Maybe it didn't start out that way, maybe they did love one another once.' Hattie wondered if he was simply trying to backtrack at the look of devastation she couldn't hide. She'd built up a world in her head of Roman's life now, one of love and happiness, one she'd put there to stop herself from hating him, and with just a few words it collapsed.

'Oh, Hattie.' Jensen started to move again, leading her once more in a slow sway in time with the music. 'Have you been carrying that guilt with you all this time?'

She licked her lips, feeling her own brows pulling down into scowl. She always wore her emotions on her sleeve Victoria was always telling her. She needed to control them better or the world would use them against her.

'Hey.' He took a hand from her waist and gently lifted her chin. When she still didn't meet his gaze, he ducked his head to hers. '*You* didn't do anything wrong. My brother can be a dick. He gets it from our father.'

'What about your mother?'

'Nicest woman you'll ever meet. Poor taste in men. Roman's her favourite.' A giggle slipped from Hattie's lips. 'Attagirl,' Jensen said as he suddenly turned her and dipped her low. She laughed again, holding on to his arm, frightened he might drop her, but she knew he never would.

His face lost all trace of amusement, his eyes far more serious than she'd ever seen them. They almost reminded her of Roman's…

'I hope you don't mind,' Jensen murmured as he slowly brought her back to her feet. 'But I'm going to kiss you now, Henrietta.'

ALSO BY E.V. DARCY

The Royals of Avalone - Inheritance:Victoria
Buying Him: Victoria Part 1
Taking Him: Victoria Part 2
Keeping Him: Victoria Part 3

The Royals of Avalone - Inheritance: Henrietta
Beating the System: Henrietta Part 1
Cheating the System: Henrietta Part 2

COMING SOON
The Royals of Avalone - Inheritance: Henrietta
Defeating the System: Henrietta Part 3

The Royals of Avalone - Inheritance: Alexandra
Becoming a Queen: Alexandra Part 1
Playing a Queen: Alexandra Part 2
Crowning a Queen: Alexandra Part 3

ABOUT THE AUTHOR

E. V. Darcy is a former high school teacher with a Bachelor of Arts in Imaginative Writing from Liverpool John Moores University.

She lives in the north of England with her husband and rather large–and very *spoilt*–dog, Jabba, who she rescued in 2015.

When Evie isn't writing you can find her binge watching her favourite T.V. shows, playing computer games, crocheting or cross stitching, or walking her much loved dog.

Visit E. V. Darcy's website for more information on her latest releases and other titbits. Join her newsletter for sneak peeks, first to know about forthcoming releases and discounts on pre-orders!

www.evdarcy.com

Other ways to contact E. V. Darcy:

- facebook.com/evdarcy
- twitter.com/eviedarcy
- instagram.com/evdarcy
- bookbub.com/authors/e-v-darcy
- goodreads.com/evdarcy